PENGUIN CLASSICS

Signed, Picpus

T0228661

'I love reading Simenon. He

'A truly wonderful writer . . . marvellously readable – lucid, simple, absolutely in tune with the world he creates'
– Muriel Spark

'Few writers have ever conveyed with such a sure touch, the bleakness of human life'
– A. N. Wilson

'One of the greatest writers of the twentieth century . . . Simenon was unequalled at making us look inside, though the ability was masked by his brilliance at absorbing us obsessively in his stories'
– *Guardian*

'A novelist who entered his fictional world as if he were part of it'
– Peter Ackroyd

'The greatest of all, the most genuine novelist we have had in literature'
– André Gide

'Superb . . . The most addictive of writers . . . A unique teller of tales'
– *Observer*

'The mysteries of the human personality are revealed in all their disconcerting complexity'
– Anita Brookner

'A writer who, more than any other crime novelist, combined a high literary reputation with popular appeal' – P. D. James

'A supreme writer . . . Unforgettable vividness'
– *Independent*

'Compelling, remorseless, brilliant'
– John Gray

'Extraordinary masterpieces of the twentieth century'
– John Banville

GEORGES SIMENON

Signed, Picpus

Translated by DAVID COWARD

PENGUIN BOOKS

PENGUIN CLASSICS

UK | USA | Canada | Ireland | Australia
India | New Zealand | South Africa

Penguin Books is part of the Penguin Random House group of companies
whose addresses can be found at global.penguinrandomhouse.com.

Penguin
Random House
UK

First published in French as *Signé Picpus* by Éditions Gallimard 1944
This translation first published 2015

012

Set in Dante MT Std 12.5/15 pt
Typeset by Palimpsest Book Production Limited, Falkirk, Stirlingshire

Printed and bound in Great Britain by Clays Ltd, Elcograf S.p.A.

ISBN: 978-0-241-18846-0

www.greenpenguin.co.uk

Contents

Signed, Picpus

1. Did Picpus Lie?

Three minutes to five. A white light flashes in the huge map of Paris which fills the whole of one wall. An operator puts down his sandwich, plugs a line jack into one of the myriad holes that is a telephone switchboard.

'Hello? Is that the fourteenth *arrondissement*? . . . Has your bus left yet?'

Maigret, trying hard to look unconcerned, with the sun full on him, wipes his forehead. The operator mutters a few monosyllables, unplugs the jack, reaches for his sandwich and murmurs for the benefit of the detective chief inspector from the Police Judiciaire:

'A Bercy!'

In the jargon, a 'Bercy' is a drunk. It is August. Paris reeks of tarmac. The noise from the Cité in the heart of Paris drifts in through the large, open windows into this room which is the nerve centre of the Police Emergency Service. Below, in the courtyard of the Préfecture de Police, two vans full of policemen are visible, ready to leave whenever the word is given.

Another light winks on, this time in the eighteenth *arrondissement*. Sausage sandwich down. Plug in.

'Hello? . . . Ah, Gérard! . . . On duty? . . . What's happening your end? . . . Right! . . . Fine! . . .'

Defenestration. It's the method of choice of poor people

who commit suicide, especially the old men and, oddly enough, especially in the eighteenth *arrondissement*. Maigret knocks out his pipe on the window-sill, refills it and glances up at the clock. Yes or no: has someone killed the clairvoyant?

The door opens. Sergeant Lucas, short, podgy, flustered. He wipes his brow too.

'Still nothing, chief?'

Like Maigret, he has just walked across the boulevard which separates the headquarters of the Police Judiciaire from the Préfecture. A neighbourly call.

'So, our man's there . . .'

'Mascouvin?'

'He's as pale as papier mâché. He's insisting on talking to you. He's saying suicide is the only way out left to him . . .'

Another light comes on. Maybe this is it? No . . . Just a brawl out at Saint-Ouen.

The phone rings. The commissioner of the Police Judiciaire, for the inspector.

'Maigret? . . . Got something? . . . *Anything?* . . .'

The irony in his voice is audible. Maigret is getting angry. He is hot. He'd give anything for a freshly drawn beer. And for the first time in his life he is almost on the point of wanting a crime, the crime he is expecting, to happen. Absolutely! If the clairvoyant is not killed at exactly five o'clock or rather, as was written on the blotting-pad, 'at five in the afternoon', then he'll have to put up with months of sarcastic smiles and jokes, some funnier than others.

'Go and bring me Mascouvin.'

God knows but the man looks like a joker! He turned

4

up the previous evening at the Police Judiciaire with gloom written all over him, and wouldn't take no for an answer, his face twitching with a nervous tic, insisting loudly on speaking to Detective Chief Inspector Maigret in person.

'It's a matter of life and death!' he said.

A small, thin man, rather dull to look at, neither young nor old, exuding the stale smell of a bachelor who does not look after himself. He pulls his fingers and cracks his knuckles while telling his tale, the way a schoolboy recites his lesson.

'Fifteen years I've worked for Proud and Drouin, property dealers on Boulevard Bonne-Nouvelle. I live alone in a two-roomed flat, 21, Place des Vosges . . . Every evening I go for a game of bridge in a club in Rue des Pyramides . . . For the last two months, I've been having a run of bad luck. I've lost all my savings . . . I owe the countess 800 francs . . .'

Maigret only half-listens, thinking that one half of the population of Paris is on holiday and that at that moment the other half is downing cold drinks under the awnings of pavement cafés. Who was this countess? Well, the sad little man explains. An upper-class lady who has been through hard times and set up a bridge club in Rue des Pyramides. A good-looking woman. It's obvious: this small dull man is in love.

'Today, at four o'clock, inspector, I took a thousand-franc note from my employers' till.'

He could not have cut a more tragic figure if he'd wiped out an entire family. He continues with his confession, still cracking his fingers. After the offices of Proud and Drouin closed for the day, he wandered around the boulevards with the thousand-franc note in his pocket. He was racked by guilt. He walked into the Café des Sports at the corner of Place de la République and Boulevard Voltaire, where he usually has a lonely drink before his evening meal.

'Can I have pen and paper, Nestor?'

For he called the waiter by his Christian name. Yes, he will write to his employers. He will confess everything and send the thousand-franc note back! His luck has deserted him for too long! He has been losing steadily for two months. The countess he silently adores only has eyes for a retired army captain and is always strict in making Mascouvin pay up what he owes her.

Surrounded by the bustling crowd, he stared at the blotting-pad which lay open in front of him. Mechanically, he had put his pince-nez down on the blotter and looked at it there with his large, short-sighted eyes. It was at that moment that the strange thing happened. One of the lenses, acting as a mirror, reflected the criss-cross, hatched ink marks which had dried on the blotter. Mascouvin made out the words: *will kill* . . . He looked more closely . . . The lens restored the original image:

Tomorrow, at five in the afternoon, I will kill . . .
Tomorrow, at five in the afternoon, I will kill the clairvoyant.
Signed, Picpus.

Five past five. The operator has had time to finish eating his sausage, which smells of garlic, for the white lights on the map of Paris have remained dormant. A sound of footsteps on the stairs. It is Lucas bringing sad little Mascouvin.

The previous evening, Maigret told him to go home, turn up for work as usual and put the thousand francs back where they belonged. As a precaution, Lucas had followed him. At about nine o'clock, Mascouvin was hanging around in Rue des Pyramides but did not go into the countess's building. He spent the night at home in Place des Vosges. Next morning he went to his office and at midday ate his lunch in a cheap café on Boulevard Saint-Martin.

Then, at four thirty, when it was all getting too much for him, he suddenly left the sombre offices of Proud and Drouin and headed off towards Quai des Orfèvres.

'I can't stand it any more, inspector . . . I daren't look my employers in the face . . . It seems like . . .'

'Sit down . . . Don't say anything . . .'

Eight minutes past five! A glorious sun lights up the teeming streets of Paris; the men are in shirt-sleeves and the women are almost naked under their light dresses. Meanwhile, the police are keeping watch on eighty-two clairvoyants, some more far-sighted than others.

'You don't think, Maigret, it could be a hoax?'

Lucas is worried about his chief, who stands to make himself a laughing-stock. A light goes in the third *arrondissement*.

'Hello? . . . Right . . . Fine . . .'

The operator turns to Maigret and sighs:

'Another Bercy . . . But it's not Saturday . . .'

Mascouvin, unable to stop fidgeting and pulling his fingers, opens his mouth:

'Excuse me, sir . . . I'd just like to say . . .'

'Well don't!' snarls Maigret, shutting him up.

Come on, yes or no, is this Picpus going to make up his mind and kill himself a clairvoyant?

The light of the eighteenth *arrondissement* again.

'Hello? . . . Detective Chief Inspector Maigret? . . . I'll put him on . . .'

Maigret's heart misses a beat as he grabs the receiver.

'Hello . . . Yes . . . The station in Rue Damrémont? . . . Say again? . . . 67A, Rue Coulaincourt . . . Mademoiselle Jeanne? . . . A clairvoyant?'

His voice is loud and urgent. His face lights up.

'Come on, look lively! . . . Lucas, take him back . . . You never know . . .'

Joseph Mascouvin, like a sleepwalker, the lugubrious kind of sleepwalker, follows the two men down the dusty stairs. A police car is waiting in the courtyard.

'67A, Rue Coulaincourt . . . And step on it . . .'

On the way, Maigret flicks through the list of clairvoyants and fortune-tellers which had been drawn up the evening before. He had ordered a discreet watch to be kept on them . . . Of course, Mademoiselle Jeanne's name is not on it! . . .

'Faster!'

And now this clown Mascouvin asks timidly:

'Is she dead?'

For a moment, Maigret wonders if he is as simple-minded as he looks. He'll find out sooner or later!

'Gun?' whispers Lucas.

'Knife.'

There is no need to look at the numbers on the houses. Just opposite Place Constantin-Pecqueur, a small crowd identifies the house where the crime has just occurred.

'Shall I wait for you?' stammers Mascouvin.

'Come inside with us . . . Come along! Keep up!'

The uniformed policemen give way to let Maigret and Sergeant Lucas through.

'Fifth floor. On your right.'

No lift. The house is clean, quite comfortable. Tenants out on the landings, all as it should be. On the fifth floor, the police chief in charge of the eighteenth *arrondissement* precinct holds out his hand to Maigret.

'Come in . . . It's only just happened . . . Stroke of luck that we were informed so soon, as you'll see.'

They walk into virtually full sunlight. The small living room has a bay window, now wide open, which leads out to a balcony with a view over the city. The room is daintily stylish, hushed, with light-coloured curtains, Louis XVI armchairs, tasteful curios and knick-knacks. A local doctor straightens up.

'There's nothing I can do . . . The second thrust of the knife was the one that killed her . . .'

The room is too small for the number of people now in it. After filling his pipe, Maigret takes off his jacket and reveals a pair of mauve braces which his wife bought for him the previous week. The police chief smiles at the sight of the braces, which, even more extravagantly, are made of silk. Maigret scowls.

'So? . . . What have you got? . . . I haven't got all day . . .'

'Well. I haven't had time to gather much information, not

least because the concierge isn't the chatty sort. You have to dig words out of her, like pulling teeth . . . A Mademoiselle Jeanne, real name Marie Picard, born Bayeux . . .'

Maigret has raised the sheet which has been thrown over the body. Fine-looking woman, and no mistake. Fortyish. Well upholstered, well groomed, hair blonde but maybe not naturally so?

'She wasn't registered as a medium and didn't advertise. But she had regular customers, most of them quite well-heeled apparently, who used to come here to consult her . . .'

'How many clients did she see this afternoon?'

'The concierge, Madame Baffoin, Eugénie Baffoin, doesn't know. She reckons it's none of her business. Says not all concierges are as nosy as they are made out to be. At a few minutes after five, this lady here . . .'

A small, brisk woman, also middle-aged, gets to her feet. The hat she is wearing is a touch ridiculous. She explains:

'I knew Mademoiselle Jeanne. She used to come down to Morsang sometimes for a few days. Do you know Morsang? . . . It's on the Seine, just upstream from Corbeil, where the dam is . . . I run the inn there, the Beau Pigeon . . . Isidore had been out fishing, he caught some fine tench, and since I was coming to Paris anyway, I thought . . .'

The tench, wrapped in green leaves, still fresh, are there, in a basket.

'Well, I knew she'd be pleased, for she did like her fish . . .'

'Had you known Mademoiselle Jeanne long?'

'Maybe five years or so? . . . One time she stayed with us for a month . . .'

'Alone?'

'What do you take her for? . . . Anyway, I popped in here while I was doing my shopping . . . The door wasn't shut . . . Being as it was half open, I called: "Mademoiselle Jeanne! . . . It's just me, Madame Roy . . ." Then, since there was no answer, I came in . . . She was sitting at that little table, bent over. Tell the truth, I thought she was sleeping . . . I put my hand out to shake her and . . .'

So at about seven minutes past five, Mademoiselle Jeanne, a clairvoyant, was already dead from two stab wounds in the back.

'Has the weapon been found?' asks Maigret, turning to the police chief.

'No.'

'Any furniture broken?'

'Nothing . . . No signs of a struggle . . . It doesn't seem as if the murderer went into the bedroom . . . This way . . .'

He opens a door. The bedroom is as cheerful as the living room. A genuine boudoir, all light colours. The nest of a flirtatious woman who likes her comfort.

'And you say the concierge . . .'

'Claims she doesn't know anything . . . Madame Roy went down to the bar next door to phone us. We found her waiting downstairs, by the door. There's just one detail . . . Hold on, here's the locksmith I sent for . . . In here, please . . . Open this door, would you?'

Maigret happens to look up and sees Mascouvin sitting on the edge of his chair. The clerk from Proud and Drouin says:

'I feel as if my heart's giving out, inspector . . .'

'That's too bad!'

Later, when the people from the prosecutor's office and the specialist team from Criminal Records show up, it will get a lot worse! If only Maigret had time for a beer in the Café Manière!

'As you can see,' the police chief is telling him, 'the apartment has this living room, a rustic-style dining room there, the bedroom, a box-room and . . .'

He nods towards a door where the locksmith is at work.

'I assume it's the kitchen . . .'

A master-key turns in the lock. The door opens.

'Huh! . . . What are you doing in there? . . . Who are you? . . .'

It's so unexpected it's almost comic. In a small, spotlessly neat kitchenette, where no plates or dirty glasses have been left lying about, what is revealed but an old man perched on the edge of the table, solemnly waiting.

'Speak up! . . . What are you doing here?'

The elderly gent stares in bewilderment at the two men who are challenging him and finds nothing to say. The oddest thing is that in the middle of August he is enveloped in a greenish overcoat. His cheeks are hidden by an ill-kempt beard. He looks away, his shoulders droop.

'How long have you been here, in this kitchen?'

He concentrates, as if he hasn't quite understood, then takes out his pocket-watch and opens the front.

'Forty minutes,' he says eventually.

'So that means you were here at five o'clock?'

'I got here before that . . .'

'Were you here when the crime was committed?'

'What crime?'

He is hard of hearing and leans his head towards his interrogator the way deaf people do.

'You mean you don't know that . . .'

The sheet over the corpse is lifted. The old man stares in amazement and stands rooted to the spot.

'Well?'

He does not answer. He wipes his eyes. But it doesn't necessarily mean that he's crying, for Maigret has already observed that his eyes were watery to start with.

'What were you doing in the kitchen?'

He stares at them again. It's as if words have no meaning for him.

'How is it that you were locked inside the kitchen?' he is asked again. 'The key wasn't on the inside. It isn't outside either . . .'

'I don't know . . .' he whispers quietly, like a child who's afraid of getting the stick.

'What don't you know?'

'Nothing.'

'Have you got any papers?'

He searches through his pockets, awkwardly, wipes his eyes again, sniffles, and finally hands over a wallet with initials on it picked out in silver. The police chief and Maigret exchange looks.

Is this old man really senile or is he acting a role and

doing it to perfection? From the wallet, Maigret takes out an identity card and reads it aloud.

'Octave Le Cloaguen, retired ship's doctor, age: sixty-eight, 13, Boulevard des Batignolles, Paris.'

'Clear the room!' Maigret barks suddenly.

Joseph Mascouvin gets meekly to his feet.

'Not you . . . Stay here, dammit! . . . And sit down!'

It is literally stifling for the ten or fifteen people in this doll-sized flat.

'You sit down too, Monsieur Le Cloaguen! . . . And you can begin by telling me what you were doing in this house.'

Le Cloaguen gives a start. He has heard the sound of the words but has not understood their meaning. Maigret repeats his question and is obliged to shout.

'Oh, yes! . . . Sorry . . . I'd come . . .'

'To do what?'

'To see her . . .' he stammered, motioning to the body under the sheet.

'You wanted to know what the future has in store for you?'

No reply.

'Tell me, were you, yes or no, one of her clients? . . .'

'Yes . . . I'd come . . .'

'And what happened?'

'I was sitting here . . . Yes, on this gilt chair . . . Someone knocked on the door . . . Like this . . .'

He goes to the door. It seems possible that he intends to run off. But no, it's only to knock in a particular, jerky way.

'Then, *she* said . . .'

'All right, tell us . . . What did she say?'

'She said: "Quick, in here!" . . . and she pushed me into the kitchen . . .'

'Was she the one who locked you in?'

'I don't know.'

'What happened then?'

'Nothing . . . I sat on the table . . . The window was open . . . I looked out into the street . . .'

'After that?'

'After that, nothing . . . A lot of people came . . . I didn't think I should show my face . . .'

He speaks quietly, slowly, almost ruefully and then suddenly asks a very unexpected question:

'You wouldn't have any tobacco on you?'

'Cigarette?'

'Tobacco.'

'You smoke a pipe?'

Maigret holds out his pouch. Le Cloaguen takes a twist of tobacco and puts it in his mouth with visible satisfaction.

'There's no point telling my wife . . .'

Meanwhile, Lucas has been searching the flat. Maigret knows exactly what he is looking for.

'Well?'

'Nothing, sir . . . The key to the kitchen isn't anywhere here . . . I also asked an officer to go down and take a look around in the street, in case it was thrown out of the window . . .'

Maigret sums up, for the benefit of Le Cloaguen:

'So in short, you say you got here just before five to consult the clairvoyant. At two or three minutes to five, someone knocked on the door in a distinctive way, and

Mademoiselle Jeanne pushed you into the kitchen . . . Have I got that right? . . . You looked out at the street, then you heard voices and you didn't move a muscle . . . You didn't even look through the keyhole.'

'No . . . I thought she was entertaining visitors . . .'

'You've been before?'

'Every week.'

'Over a long period?'

'Very long.'

Gaga or not gaga?

There is great excitement in the neighbourhood. More than 200 people have collected in the street below by the time the vehicles bringing the prosecutor's people arrive. Outside are sunshine, bright colours, café terraces where it is very pleasant to sit in front of a cold beer. Maigret puts his jacket back on because the important gentlemen are coming up the stairs.

'Ah! It's you, detective chief inspector,' says the deputy public prosecutor. 'Am I to understand that we have an interesting case here?'

'Yes, apart from the fact that so far I'm having to deal with two lunatics!' Maigret mutters to himself.

First the moron Mascouvin, who never takes his eyes off Maigret's bulky figure! And then there's this old man who chews tobacco and sniffles!

More cars arrive. This time, it's the journalists.

'Listen, Lucas . . . Get these two characters out of here . . . I'll be back at headquarters in half an hour.'

It is then that Mascouvin comes out with a priceless remark.

After shaking his head and looking for his hat all round the living room, which is now a mess, he murmurs with the seriousness with which he does everything:

'You do realize, inspector,' he observes, 'that it was Picpus who killed the clairvoyant!'

2. The Sweating Man

Curiously enough, it was as he sat staring mechanically at a hand, a man's hand on a knee covered by worn cloth, that Maigret all at once felt in some way involved in what had happened and stopped thinking of the man at his side as just another regular customer, though a somewhat colourful one.

Back there in Rue Coulaincourt, it had been a circus, to use Maigret's word for it. He hated being descended on by the public prosecutor's officers. In the mêlée, the inspector had thought that Octave Le Cloaguen had looked like a cranky old man who seemed permanently bewildered. At the very most, Maigret had been intrigued by the vacant stare which suddenly came over his pale eyes, as if his soul had momentarily been transported elsewhere. A question would be put to him two, three times, eventually the words would finally sink in, and he would furrow his brow as he tried to understand.

Later, at Quai des Orfèvres, in his office which the sun had turned into a Turkish bath, a perspiring Maigret, repeatedly mopping his face, had questioned him thoroughly, but the results were more or less unhelpful. Le Cloaguen never got flustered. He even gave the impression that he was trying his best to please the inspector. And whereas Maigret kept wiping his forehead and the back of his neck with his handkerchief, the old man's skin stayed perfectly dry, despite the overcoat which he had not taken off. Maigret had taken note: it confirmed his suspicion.

And now both men were being driven along in an open taxi. It was eight in the evening, and the streets of Paris were filled with a pleasant coolness. Le Cloaguen did not move, and Maigret, without thinking of anything in particular, was staring at the old man's right hand, which was resting on his knee, a strangely long hand with gnarled joints and skin so parchment-like that in places it looked as if it might split, like dried-up bark. The top of the index finger was missing.

Was it this hand . . . ? Maigret's mind was working . . . A hand could do so many things in the course of a lifetime, and what over a period of sixty-seven years had this hand . . . ?

Suddenly a drop of water landed on the taut skin and scattered. At that point, they were driving along Rue de Wagram, a street lined on both sides by cafés and cinemas, through the happy noise and bustle of the crowds. Maigret looked up. The man was looking straight ahead of him, his features as stiff as ever, but a fringe of sweat had spread across his forehead.

It was so unexpected that the inspector was disconcerted. Why, when he had kept his almost exaggerated composure for so long, was Le Cloaguen now suddenly showing symptoms of panic? For there could be no mistaking the signs. The perspiration had not been brought on by the heat, but by fear, that ignoble inward disintegration which cannot be resisted.

Had the old man seen something? Or someone? Unlikely. Was it having a policeman's eyes staring at his hand that had unsettled him? Could the missing finger joint possibly be some sort of clue?

They soon reached Boulevard de Courcelles and were travelling past the gilded gates and blue-black shadows of Parc Monceau when Maigret finally understood, for the sweat was pouring off the forehead of the man at his side, and his face had acquired a pasty look: *what was causing his panic was the fact that he was getting nearer to his house.*

A few minutes more and they were on Boulevard des Batignolles. A house built of grey stone. An imposing entrance. A well-to-do, even affluent look about it. The concierge's lodge was well kept, and its occupant was trimly dressed in black. The stairs were dark, varnished and covered with a scarlet runner held in place by brass rods.

Le Cloaguen climbed up them slowly, gasping for breath and, though he did not speak, his forehead still streamed with sweat. What was he afraid of?

A single door on each floor, large doors made of dark oak with highly polished brass fittings. When they reached the third floor, Maigret rang the bell. For a whole minute, which seemed very long, a sound of furtive steps came from inside the apartment, until finally the door half opened and remained only half-open, and a woman's face appeared. It wore a curious, suspicious expression.

'Madame Le Cloaguen, I presume?'

To which she replied very quickly:

'The maid's gone out . . . I myself had to . . .'

Maigret sensed that she was lying. At that moment, he would have sworn she did not have a maid.

'I would like very much, if it's not too much trouble, to talk to you for a few moments . . . Detective Chief Inspector Maigret, Police Judiciaire . . .'

The woman, who was probably about fifty years of age, short, apprehensive, with a face that was too mobile and remarkably vivacious eyes, looked at her husband. This lasted just a few seconds. Once again, Maigret had the impression of being able to detect the smell of fear in the air.

Le Cloaguen's face was expressionless. He did not say anything and explained nothing. He just stood there, his inner being again transported to some other place, waiting on the doormat to go into his apartment.

The woman, who had regained her composure, stepped to one side then took a few steps back and opened the door of an immense drawing room into which thick curtains allowed only a dim grey light to pass.

'Please be seated . . . What is it . . . ? . . . What has he . . . ?'

Another brief look at her husband, to whom it had not occurred to remove his overcoat or take off his hat.

Ten years hence, Maigret would still be able to reconstitute this drawing room down to the smallest details and picture the three tall windows hung with green velvet curtains with yellow tassels, antique chairs covered with dust-sheets, the small gilt table, the large mirror with dulled silvering above the black marble fireplace, the brass fire dogs . . .

A faint rustling from behind a door. Someone was there,

listening, a presence which Maigret had the impression was female; and he was not wrong: very soon he would learn that it was Gisèle Le Cloaguen, unmarried, aged twenty-eight.

The apartment seemed to be very big, for it occupied the whole of one floor. Certain things suggested money but others had an odour of poverty. Madame Le Cloaguen was dressed in black silk and had fine rings on her fingers and a gold-mounted cameo brooch on her breast.

'Could I start, madame, by asking if you are acquainted with someone called Mademoiselle Jeanne?'

He was sure she wasn't. But she ransacked her memory, obviously having expected an entirely different question.

'What does this person do?'

'She lives in Rue Coulaincourt . . .'

'I don't see . . .'

'She earned her living by predicting the future . . . I can tell you what this is all about in a few words . . . Briefly then, this person was murdered at home today, at five o'clock . . . Now it so happens that at that time your husband was present in the apartment, where he was found locked inside the kitchen . . .'

'Octave, tell me what . . .'

She had turned to face him and spoke calmly and with dignity and yet she gave the impression that the calmness and dignity were no more genuine that the bronze andirons in the fireplace. Maigret was convinced that, if he got up and left, the door would scarcely have closed behind him before a sordid scene would erupt between the pair of them.

Before replying, Le Cloaguen had to swallow his saliva.

'I was there,' he said, looking humble and defeated.

She replied with haughty disdain:

'I had no idea you were in the habit of having your fortune told!'

Then she suddenly lost interest in him, sat down opposite Maigret and, in her best society manner, played absently with her cameo and began speaking with increasing volubility.

'I must tell you now, inspector. I know nothing about this business. But I do know my husband. As he may have told you, he spent a long time working as a doctor on board liners sailing on South American routes. For several years he also sailed the China seas. Since then, alas, he has not been a man like other men . . .'

She was not in the least inhibited by the presence of Le Cloaguen.

'You must surely have noticed that he has become like a child again . . . It's most unfortunate for my daughter and myself for it has caused serious harm to our social life.'

Maigret looked around at the sitting room and in his mind's eye imagined the receptions given here on Boulevard des Batignolles, the armchairs with their dust-sheets removed, the chandelier lit up, petits fours on the round gilt table, very stiff-backed ladies simpering over the tea cups.

Later, the concierge would confirm what he was thinking. She would tell him about the weekly receptions, the 'Mondays', as everyone in the house sarcastically called them.

It was also true that the Le Cloaguens had no maid, that a charwoman came every morning but on Mondays a head waiter was hired from Potel and Chabot.

'And them being so well off!' would add the concierge, who was far more forthcoming than the one in Rue Coulaincourt. 'People reckon they've got more than 200,000 francs a year coming in. A notary from Saint-Raphaël travels up special once a year, in December, to bring them the money. Makes you wonder what they do with it. The shopkeepers hereabouts will tell you. In the butcher's they only ask for the cheapest cuts, and you wouldn't call the amounts they buy large. You've seen for yourself how the poor husband is dressed, winter and summer . . .'

But what connection was there between this apartment and the light, airy flat in Rue Coulaincourt? Between this thin, tautly strung, so frighteningly self-controlled woman, and the pampered and cosseted Mademoiselle Jeanne, who had died in her living room full of sunshine?

The investigation had only just begun. Maigret was trying not to draw conclusions from what he was seeing and hearing. He preferred to imagine people in their contexts: like the strange Mascouvin, at his desk at Proud and Drouin's, then at home on Place des Vosges, or even in the countess's bridge club in Rue des Pyramides.

'Just like a big, overgrown child, inspector, I can't find any other word for him . . . He spends every day wandering around the streets and only comes home for his meals . . . But I can assure you that he is perfectly harmless . . .'

Harmless! . . . The word struck Maigret. He looked up at the old man. The sweat had vanished from his forehead, and he just sat where he was, quite unconcerned by what was going on around him.

What had he been afraid of? Why had he got his self-assurance back? Or rather his indifference?

There was another scuffle at the door, and Madame Le Cloaguen said in a clear voice:

'You can come in, Gisèle . . . May I introduce my daughter? She's the one really who's been hit hardest by her father's condition . . . You must understand . . . When she invites friends here . . .'

Why did Gisèle dress so badly and why did she choose to look so sour-faced when otherwise she could have been pretty? She shook hands like a man. Not a smile, nothing warm in her greeting. Such pitiless severity in the look she turned on the old man.

It was she who told him, as if she were speaking to a servant:

'Go and take your coat and hat off.'

'Would you believe, Gisèle,' explained her mother, 'that this afternoon your father went to see a fortune-teller and as it happens there's been a scandal . . .'

Curious to hear the word 'scandal' being applied to a crime! It was patently obvious that the life or death of Mademoiselle Jeanne meant little to these women. What mattered was that Le Cloaguen had been there, that he'd been marched off to Quai des Orfèvres and that now, a detective chief inspector . . .

'I'm very sorry, ladies, to bother you like this but, given the circumstances, I'd be glad if I could have a look round Monsieur Le Cloaguen's room . . .'

'Gisèle?' murmured Madame Le Cloaguen, as though it were a question.

The young woman blinked, which doubtless meant that the room had been tidied.

To reach it, they had first to walk through a comfortable dining room, then a bedroom, which belonged to the mistress of the household and contained antique furniture, among which were some rather fine pieces. Maigret noted the fact that there was no bathroom in the apartment, only small rooms with wash-basins in which the wallpaper had not been changed for some considerable time and the floor was covered by odd pieces of linoleum.

'His room doubles as an office,' said the wife. 'He has clung to the habit of simplicity, great simplicity, which he acquired during his travels . . .'

Well! Why was the bolt on the outside of the door not on the inside, which would have been more logical? Did the old man get shut up in his room?

On this point too Maigret's intuition would be confirmed by the concierge.

'Oh yes, sir . . . When the ladies have visitors the old man is shut in because they are so terrified he'll suddenly barge in on them . . . If he gets back late for his dinner, he gets punished by being locked up for a day or two . . .'

A closet rather than a room, looking out, not on to Boulevard des Batignolles but on a dark, narrow courtyard. Even then the windows were covered with an opaque adhesive film which made it even dimmer inside.

A naked, dusty 25-candle-power bulb dangled from an electric wire. An iron bed. A three-legged washstand and a chipped ewer on the floor. In a corner, the item of furniture which justified the grandiose name of office given to the room: a desk made of dark wood, a huge affair and much too big for the space available, doubtless bought second-hand at a public auction.

Le Cloaguen had come back to his room without making a sound and now stood waiting, the way a schoolboy waits for the inevitable cane. Soon Maigret would go and then . . .

The inspector felt almost guilty at the thought of leaving him alone with these two women. He remembered the hand with the missing finger joint, an old hand which . . .

'Spartan, isn't it?' remarked Madame Le Cloaguen, pleased to have come up with the word. 'He has only to say and he could have a much more comfortable room, but he does like his simplicity. And it's he who insists on wearing that old overcoat winter and summer. You couldn't persuade him to do otherwise for all the tea in China . . .'

And what about the kitchen, madame? Is he also the one who insists that it should be in such a mess, with a pile of dirty dishes on a wobbly table, pans that never get scoured, empty cupboards, a few withered vegetables left to fester and the coagulated remains of a stew which will presumably be served up for dinner?

Gisèle's room is exactly like her mother's: comfortable, well-furnished, but with the same oppressive, antiquated feel to it.

And to think that outside, the whole of Paris is making the most of a fine August evening, enjoying a sun that sets in a purple haze and coolness which is to be savoured like a fragrant sorbet, and that here, not two minutes from the world's most exciting streets, these people live in a kind of necropolis!

'Have you lived long in this apartment?'

'Ten years, inspector. Ever since we left Saint-Raphaël. It's especially since then that my husband has gone into a decline. In fact, it was to get better treatment for him that we moved to Paris.'

Now that was, at the very least, strange! As if there weren't enough notable doctors on the Côte d'Azur! As if the hustle and bustle of Paris could be of any help in recovering a poor man's wits!

Le Cloaguen has remained in his room the way a well-trained dog stays in its kennel when there are visitors. Maigret would like to see him again, talk to him. 'Fellow-feeling' is not quite the correct expression. Yet he is drawn to the man, he feels he is beginning to understand him, or rather to glimpse something of the mystery of his wretched existence.

The wife on the other hand is as transparent as before.

'As you see, there are no mysteries in our home, and if my husband took it into his head to have his fortune told, then . . . But can we ever know what goes on in enfeebled minds? . . . I do hope, inspector, that it won't be long before the murderer is found and that this dreadful business will not have any consequences . . .'

Consequences for whom exactly? For her, of course! For her and for her daughter, who is so like her that they form a single entity!

In fact, what is it that is missing in this apartment? Two

or three times, Maigret has had the impression of an absence, as when a familiar object has been moved from its place. Yet all the usual pieces of furniture are there. He looks around him, feeling tense as people do when there is something they just can't put their finger on . . .

'I'll say good evening, inspector. If there's anything else you'd like to know . . .'

What will happen once the door is closed? He walks down the stairs. He can't help thinking about the man in his room, about the woman who bursts in, fuming, her face twisted by anger, by fury . . .

And then it suddenly strikes him. What was absent from the apartment, the thing that had given him the impression of something missing, was that he had seen no photographs anywhere on the walls or furniture! Nothing! Not even one of those enlargements you find in the lowliest homes, no amateur snaps, souvenirs of holidays on beaches or in the mountains.

Bare walls, implacably bare!

Maigret spends a quarter of an hour in the concierge's lodge, then finds himself once more on the pavement. Inspector Janvier approaches.

'What do you want me to do, chief?'

'Stay here . . . I'd be curious to know what those people . . .'

When he gets to Place Clichy, he walks into a bar, phones Madame Maigret to say he doesn't know when he'll be home and finally sits down with a beer in front of him.

The business of the key is bizarre. Did Mademoiselle Jeanne, when she pushed the old man into the kitchen –

always assuming that what Le Cloaguen's said is true – lock him in?

Really, it looks as if the old man is fated to keep getting himself locked up, the proof being the bolt fixed outside his room on Boulevard des Batignolles . . .

But who removed the key? The murderer? So did he know there was somebody on the other side of the door?

Earlier, Maigret had blundered when he looked around the apartment in Rue Coulaincourt. Had there been a hat in the clairvoyant's living room? It was possible, probable even. Finding himself alone with a woman, Le Cloaguen would have certainly taken his hat off. If it was left in the room, the murderer could have seen it and taken the key out of the kitchen door . . .

Now, when they had found the former ship's doctor in the clairvoyant's kitchen, did he have his hat with him?

Maigret took his notebook out of his pocket and wrote down the word *hat*.

He should have questioned everyone who had been there. But in all the excitement of the first hours of an investigation . . .

Le Cloaguen could have locked himself in and got rid of the key by throwing it out of the window or by dropping it down the lavatory.

'Here's to him!' Maigret growls, finishing a second beer. He hesitates between taking a bus or a taxi.

The bustle in the streets around him seems slightly unreal now. The Rue Coulaincourt mystery is slowly getting under his skin. The streetlamps come on, passers-by are not much more than blue shadows against a lighter blue background.

'Quai des Orfèvres . . .'

'Right you are, Monsieur Maigret!'

It's childish, but it's human: it pleases him that the driver recognizes him and gives him a friendly word.

Signed, Picpus.

To whom had the note written by an unknown man or woman in the Café des Sports on Place de la République been addressed? Isn't it strange that Joseph Mascouvin, the scrupulously honest clerk who had just, for the first time in his life, stolen a thousand francs from his employers, should ask for writing materials, put his pince-nez down on the blotter and become interested in ink stains?

'So, Monsieur Maigret, hunting big game, are we?'

Maigret sighs, pays the taxi, walks heavily up the steps of the Police Judiciaire building. François, the aged doorman, doesn't even give him time to go up to his office.

'They're waiting for you, detective chief inspector . . .'

A swift glance at the commissioner's baize door. Maigret gets the message.

The lamp with a green shade on the desk is lit, but the curtains have not been drawn. The windows are wide open and give on to a vista of wharves. Waves of cool, damp air waft into the room at intervals.

The commissioner of the Police Judiciaire looks up. Lucas is standing next to him, a Lucas who averts his eyes and looks like a whipped cur.

'It's you who's got it right, Maigret . . . It was obviously this Picpus who killed the clairvoyant . . .'

The inspector scowls. He does not see where this pre-amble might be leading.

'Unfortunately, it will be several days before the main suspect can be questioned . . .'

Why does Maigret have a sudden sinking feeling? He's only known Octave Le Cloaguen for a few hours. Can he even claim to know him? The serious expression on the commissioner's face . . . Lucas's embarrassment . . . Maigret scents trouble . . . Has the old man . . . ?

Lucas mutters:

'It's my fault.'

When are they going to come to the point?

'I questioned him for a good hour . . .'

Ah! This isn't about the former ship's doctor . . . It's about Mascouvin. Lucas had been told to question him again.

'I was intending to take him to Rue des Pyramides. It was worth a go. I thought that if I brought him face to face with his famous countess, I might get something out of him. Up to that point, he'd been quiet as a lamb. I wondered for a moment about taking a taxi. But there weren't any on the Quai. We started making for the Pont-Neuf. There were lots of people about. The Belle Jardinière had just closed and hundreds of counter staff and other employees . . .'

'And then?'

'It happened so fast that I didn't have time to stop him . . . Suddenly he jumped clean over the parapet of the bridge . . .'

Maigret fills his pipe and says nothing.

'He didn't have a chance . . . Before entering the water, he hit one of the piers . . .'

All too easy to picture the scene in the glorious evening light: hundreds, thousands of people leaning over the parapet and lining both banks, something floating, a grey hat, a dark shape re-emerging from time to time, an onlooker takes off his coat and dives in . . .

'A tug happened to be passing and . . .'

The crowd watching the scene unfold holds its collective breath. The tug manoeuvres, the propeller thrashes water streaked with red reflections of the sun, a boathook is held out to the rescuer, and at last Mascouvin, an inert Mascouvin, is hauled up the black iron hull of the boat.

'He's not dead, but he's as good as . . . His skull struck the stone work . . . He's been taken to hospital, the Hôtel-Dieu, and it's Chesnard, their top surgeon who . . .'

Maigret strikes a match and puffs on his pipe.

'What do you make of it?' asks the commissioner. 'Wouldn't you say that this changes everything?'

'Changes what exactly?' growls the inspector.

Can anyone know anything at the start of an investigation? Mademoiselle Jeanne . . . She at least is dead, there's nothing more certain in this whole business . . . Stabbed twice in the back, died as she was quietly leaning over her Louis XV table . . . Obviously she suspected nothing . . .

Le Cloaguen in the kitchen . . . Mascouvin and his countess . . .

'What's been done about the woman?' asks Maigret drawing on his pipe.

'What woman?'

'The one from Morsang . . . What's her name again? Landlady of the Beau Pigeon . . .'

'She had a train to catch . . .'

'Anyone ask if she knew Mascouvin?'

A woebegone Lucas replies:

'I didn't think to . . . She was in a hurry. It seems their inn is full . . .'

The proof that Maigret always thinks of everything is that he now mutters, and it brings a smile to the commissioner's lips:

'What happened to the tench?'

Anyone would have thought he was intending to take them home to Madame Maigret for their supper.

3. The Girl in the Red Hat

Every quarter of an hour or so, Maigret, grunting and blowing, strove as mightily as if he were trying to move a mountain, but it was only himself he was trying to free from the clammy sheets, just long enough to turn over from one side on to the other and sink back into a sleep full of nightmarish shapes. And every time it happened, Madame Maigret would wake up and, taking as always a long time to get back to sleep, would fix her eyes on the blind which swelled in the breeze like a balloon.

It was a crystal-clear night. It was so clear that from here on Boulevard Richard Lenoir you could hear, or thought you could, the rumble of activity coming from the markets of Les Halles.

A window was also open at 21, Place des Vosges, but there was no one in the room, no one on the bed, though the concierge had made it up.

In a room at the Hôtel-Dieu, a nurse with horsey features was knitting at the bedside of Joseph Mascouvin, whose face was mostly hidden by bandages.

No one was sitting up with Mademoiselle Jeanne, presently lying in an icy drawer of her own in the Forensic Institute. On Boulevard des Batignolles, near Place Clichy, Inspector Janvier got up off his bench from time to time, walked a few steps under the trees and watched the moon loom up between two gable ends covered with advertisements, and then the unlit windows of number 13.

At first, women had approached him in the dark – it was an odd thing, that evening in that part of town they were all very tall – but they soon understood and now they kept their distance, they became fewer, and the bars closed one after the other while a sudden coolness, long before a paling of the sky, indicated that the new day was not far away.

In Rue des Pyramides, in the countess's club rooms, the last of the gamblers did not leave until five in the morning, after staying themselves with sandwiches.

The papers were rolling off the presses. The iron gates of the Métro stations were being rolled back, gas was being lit under percolators and in cafés counters were piled high with warm croissants.

Torrence, still heavy with sleep, ran his eyes along Boulevard des Batignolles, looking for his colleague whom he had come to replace.

'Anything?'

'Nothing.'

Maigret, in his shirtsleeves, was having breakfast. Life was beginning to flow again in the streets, where a luminous mist still lingered.

Having tidied her flat – two rooms plus kitchen – in the district of Les Ternes, the girl in the red hat walked down the street, heading towards the Métro, and bought her usual morning paper on the way.

Instead of going to the travel agency on Boulevard de la Madeleine where she worked, she continued on to Châtelet and, her mind in a ferment and her lips trembling as if she were mumbling prayers of supplication, made her way towards the gloomy buildings of the Palais de Justice.

Maigret was in his office, standing in front of the window, busily cleaning both his pipes.

'There's a young woman asking for you. She hasn't given her name. She says it's very important . . .'

And that was how, that morning, Saturday morning, the drama resumed. The young woman was wearing a navy-blue suit and a red hat. Normally, she would have been all smiles, with dimples in her cheeks and one in her chin, but her distress changed all that.

'Where is he, inspector? . . . Is he dead? . . . He's my brother, or rather half-brother . . .'

She was talking about Mascouvin, whose picture was on the front page of her paper, next to one of Maigret, the same photograph which for more than fifteen years the newspapers always used whenever there was a new case.

'Hello? . . . Hôtel-Dieu? . . .'

No, Mascouvin wasn't dead. They were expecting at any moment the consultant who would examine him again. The patient was still in a coma, and no visitors were allowed.

'Tell me about your half-brother, mademoiselle . . . Mademoiselle who, may I ask?'

'Berthe . . . Berthe Janiveau. Everyone calls me Mademoiselle Berthe. I work as a shorthand typist in a travel agent's. My father was a joiner in a village in the Oise. I was born when my parents were quite old. They'd stopped hoping they could have a child of their own and had adopted a boy from the local orphanage, Joseph Mascouvin . . .'

Next to this fresh-faced young woman, Maigret looks like a fond, indulgent old father.

'Tell me . . . Would you mind coming with me to your brother's apartment in Place des Vosges?'

He takes her there in a taxi, and she talks, talks without stopping, so that he has no need to prompt her with questions. Inside, under the central stairwell, several women who live in the building have gathered round the concierge, who is holding a newspaper in her hand.

'Such a sober, steady man, and so polite to everybody! . . .'

The first floor is occupied by a former government minister, and the second by the owner of the building. It's only on the third floor that the visitor becomes aware of the human warmth of several families living cheek-by-jowl, ordinary folk who have rooms off both sides of a long corridor lit by the sun through a skylight.

'Why would he have wanted to do away with himself? . . . He's never had any sort of trouble in his whole life . . .'

To Maigret, Joseph Mascouvin has until now been just a rather odd, if somewhat disturbing, individual. But Mademoiselle Berthe is talking, and the apartment is also speaking: a meticulously neat room, books on serious subjects in stern bindings in a bookcase, a gramophone bought recently, a closet with a washstand and a minute kitchen.

'The truth is, inspector, he never felt he was a man like all the rest. The village children called him the kid from the orphanage. In school he was the cleverest pupil. At home, he made it a point of honour to work harder than everyone else. He was always afraid of being a nuisance, of not being wanted. He had the feeling that people only put up with him out of charity . . . My parents had to make him stay on at school . . . Then they died . . . Against all expectation, they hardly left him a thing, and because I was too young to work, it was Joseph Mascouvin who provided for me for many years . . .'

'Why weren't you still living together?'

She blushed.

'He didn't want us to . . . I mean, we weren't really brother and sister . . .'

'Tell me . . . Was your brother just a little bit in love with you?'

'I think so . . . But he never said anything . . . He wouldn't have dared . . .'

'Did he have any friends or a girlfriend?'

'Not to my knowledge . . . Sometimes we used to go out together, on a Sunday . . .'

'Did he ever take you down to Morsang?'

She tried to remember.

'Where is it?'

'It's on the Seine, upstream from Corbeil . . .'

'No . . . Most often we'd go out up the Marne, to Join-ville . . . A few months ago, Joseph got very enthusiastic about bridge . . .'

'Did he ever mention the countess?'

'Which countess?'

But though Maigret searches the room with all the

delicacy at his command, he comes up with nothing, nothing of a revelatory nature. In the desk, a number of notebooks in which Mascouvin, obsessively, kept detailed records. Books about bridge. Analyses of tricky games.

Mademoiselle Berthe points out a photo on the wall of her parents taken in front of their house which also shows her crouching at their feet.

'Do you think your half-brother was capable of stealing?'

'Stealing? Him? . . . With all his scruples?'

She laughed uncertainly.

'It's obvious you don't know him . . . I remember when for a whole week he almost made himself sick with worry because he couldn't find where he'd made a mistake of a few centimes in his accounts . . .'

'Listen to me. I advise you to go to work. As soon as there are any developments, it will be simple for us to contact you at the agency by phone . . .'

'That is a promise, isn't it, inspector? Even if I can't speak to him . . . If I could only catch a glimpse of him, just see him with my own eyes and know that he's alive . . .'

Maigret closes the window, takes one last look round the room and puts the key in his pocket. He has a quick word with the concierge. No, there was never any post for Monsieur Mascouvin. But now and then on a Saturday he used to get a pneumatic express letter from his half-sister when they were due to go out together on the Sunday. Yes, just recently the concierge noticed that he seemed preoccupied.

'Such a considerate man, inspector! . . . You know, he'd

never cross the yard without saying hello to the kids and at the end of every month he always brought them sweets . . .'

Maigret heads off on foot towards Place de la République. The Café des Sports is almost deserted. Nestor, the waiter, is wiping the imitation marble tabletops.

'Monsieur Mascouvin? I can't tell you what a shock it was when I opened the paper this morning! . . . There, that's where he always sat . . .'

A slot machine, next to the counter. At the back of the room, a Russian billiards table near which Mascouvin sat every day at the same time.

'No. I never saw him talk to anyone . . . He'd linger over his aperitif, which was always the same. He'd read his newspaper. Then he'd call me over and always gave me a twenty-five sou tip . . . When you saw him walk in, you knew almost to the minute what time it was . . .'

'Did he often ask you for pen and paper?'

'I think it was the first time . . .'

Unfortunately Nestor is unable to say if on that evening Mascouvin wrote anything or just stared at the blotter in front of him. Nor can the waiter remember who used the blotting-pad before him.

'It gets pretty busy here of an afternoon!'

Maigret sighs, mops his face and climbs on the platform of a bus and dreams listlessly of fine sand and the steady rhythm of white-crested waves.

'There's another young woman for you, Maigret. Isn't it just your lucky day!'

This time a quite different type from Mademoiselle

Berthe. A well-built girl of eighteen, by no means flat-chested, pink complexion, eyes set close to her head. Gives the impression that she's just been milking cows and smells of milk.

Actually this is more or less literally true, because she works in the dairy in Rue Coulaincourt. She is so overcome she feels she could cry.

'Monsieur Jules just said . . .'

'Excuse me? . . . Who is Monsieur Jules?'

'My boss . . . He just said I had to come to see you . . .'

She begins to get used to the atmosphere in the office and the heavy presence of the inspector, who sits there good-naturedly smoking his pipe.

'Tell me all about it.'

'I don't know what his name is, I swear! . . . It was the car I noticed more than him, a convertible, green . . .'

'But the young man . . . Describe this young man . . .'

The girl blushes. Her name is Emma, and she only came to Paris from Rouen a couple of months ago. It's her job to deliver milk to almost every house in Rue Coulaincourt. In the afternoon, she serves in the shop.

'I don't know if he's a young man. Maybe he's married? . . .'

In any case it's obvious she's in love with the man who drives the green convertible.

'He's tall, dark, very well dressed, always wears pale hats. Once he had a pair of binoculars on a strap over his shoulder . . .'

'And he always parked his car a bit lower down than number 67?'

'How do you know? . . . He'd come once a week, rarely twice . . . I'd see him go into 67A . . . I thought he must be going in to see a woman . . .'

'Why?'

'Because he was dressed like he was going to see a woman! . . . I can't explain it . . . He smelled nice . . .'

'So you passed very close to him?'

Poor Emma! You could clearly picture her at around four thirty of an afternoon watching out for the green convertible then finding an excuse to rush outside and contrive some means or other to brush past the man of her dreams!

'Did he come yesterday?'

She is on the verge of tears and says yes with a nod of her head.

'What time?'

'I don't know exactly but it was about five o'clock. He didn't stay long . . . Of course he wasn't the one who killed that woman . . .'

Is that so? Maigret questions her patiently, agreeing with whatever she says. What this brawny girl is saying is a great deal more interesting than she realizes, because the description she gives ties in to the sort of man who it is not surprising to find mixed up in this sort of case.

Too well dressed – Emma herself says it. Clothes that are too pale and always look new. A diamond ring on his finger. She also noticed that he had two gold teeth.

A regular at the races. Maigret will have to check with vice and the gambling squad. What if they came up with a man answering to his description among the countess's regulars?

43

'I am very grateful to you, mademoiselle . . . Monsieur Jules was quite right to tell you to come and see me . . .'

'He's innocent, isn't he? I can't believe that a man like him . . .'

What she doesn't say – though it is of absolutely no importance for the investigation – is that for the last few weeks every time the green convertible parks in Rue Coulaincourt, she drops a flower on the seat as she walks past!

'Did you notice anyone else going into 67A at about five o'clock?'

'A woman . . .'

'What sort of woman?'

Her description corresponds fairly closely to the landlady of the Beau Pigeon, but Emma cannot remember if the woman went into the house before or after the man in the convertible had come out.

As he speaks, Maigret jots down orders. Get an alert out for all green convertibles. Check among the racing fraternity for a man who is young, dark, etc.

'Hello? . . . Hôtel-Dieu?'

Mascouvin is not dead. The consultant in person has answered the phone. It seems the patient has a twenty per cent chance of recovering . . .

There's no way he can be questioned for a week – provided all goes well.

'Hello? Mademoiselle Berthe? Your brother will probably be all right . . . No, you can't see him yet . . . I'll keep you informed . . .'

A vast beach and the endless expanse of a mill-pond sea

. . . It's hot and Maigret sighs . . . This is the most laborious, the most discouraging time in any investigation . . . Individuals start taking shape, groups begin forming . . .

Did they lock the old man up in his room on Boulevard des Batignolles? As it happens, the answer is forthcoming. A phone call from Inspector Torrence.

'Is that you, sir? . . . I'm phoning from a little bar on the river . . . Our man left home at exactly nine o'clock . . . What? . . . Yes . . . He was indeed wearing his thick overcoat . . . No, he didn't look my way . . . He doesn't look at anything . . . He just walks straight ahead, like a convalescent out for a constitutional . . . Now and then he stops and looks in a shop window . . . He is very careful when he's crossing the road as if he's scared of the traffic . . . He hasn't turned round once . . . At the minute, he's standing behind a man fishing . . . I can see him from here . . . What's that? . . . No he hasn't spoken to anyone . . . What? I can't hear you clearly . . . Newspaper? . . . He hasn't bought a newspaper . . . Right . . . As you wish . . . Understood, I just carry on . . . I've been lucky enough to find an amazing Vouvray . . .'

Maigret makes his way solemnly, ponderously, along a service corridor to the lab located under the eaves of the Palais de Justice. He shakes hands, leans forward and peers at what the experts are doing.

'You boys come up with anything?'

Nothing interesting. The handwriting on the blotter may have been either a man's or a woman's, and there are no fingerprints on the blotting paper itself. There are many different ones on the writing pad. Just in case, they ran a check against those of known criminals but without result.

Doctor Paul, jovial as ever and extravagantly bearded, comes over in turn to say hello to the visitor.

'So there you are, Maigret! . . . Listen, about the bright spark who struck these two blows with a blade . . . The first missed the heart by a few millimetres. The second one, however, scored a direct hit on the left ventricle. I'm going to give you something to go on . . . It is not possible that the murderer, from where he was standing when he struck, could have avoided being splashed by the blood, which would have spurted out with some force . . .'

When they had found Octave Le Cloaguen in the kitchen he had no blood on his clothes, which had not been washed.

Janvier, who has had only a few hours' sleep, is back at Quai des Orfèvres.

'Take this picture, it's a photo of Mascouvin, go back to Rue Coulaincourt and show it around . . .'

He must leave no stone unturned. He can't afford to neglect any avenue . . .

'Tell me, doctor . . . Could a woman have struck those two blows?'

'Yes – if she was strong enough . . . You are aware that at certain times women, on account of their nervous constitution, can be stronger than a man . . .'

A finding unlikely to make things easier, on the contrary!

Lucas has gone off to pay a call on the countess in Rue des Pyramides. He had to wait an age because she was still in bed. She received him in a diaphanous negligée. The countess is very much the lady of quality. Uses a lorgnette. Insists on calling Lucas 'officer'.

Yes, of course, Mascouvin did owe her a small sum. Eight hundred francs? Possibly. Here we are not particularly concerned about small amounts . . . Absolutely not! She never put pressure on him to pay up . . . Poor man! . . . A wretched clerk out of his depth in a club where all the members are persons of substance: a retired colonel, the wife of a successful chocolate manufacturer, the chief clerk of a commercial bank . . . Two huge drawing rooms furnished in reasonable taste . . . In one of them a bar, and behind the bar a small galley where the sandwiches are made for patrons who stay late . . .

'Ask her,' says Maigret down the phone, 'if she knows a man who . . .'

He describes the man in the green convertible. The countess knows no one of that description.

'That you, Lucas? . . . Ask around on the street . . . Maybe someone has seen the convertible? . . .'

Maids and sales staff in shops are used to noticing models of cars that stand out from the usual run.

Coaches full of foreigners arrive in Paris in large numbers. Guides bellow into loudspeakers. The thermometer reads thirty-five degrees in the shade, and no one can dive into a swimming pool anywhere because they are all crammed with bathers standing shoulder to shoulder.

'Tell them to bring me up a beer,' Maigret orders a clerk in the Police Judiciaire. 'No, make that two . . .'

Midday. Lucas is back.

'Nothing on the green convertible . . . On the off chance, I took a copy of the list of club members. For it is a properly constituted bridge club. It doesn't seem like a lot of fun, though. The rooms have pretensions to luxury, but, to judge by the books, which are kept up to date, the games don't involve high stakes. Some members play for centimes, a few even for sous . . . Unattached people, people with no family, no friends, or husbands and wives in unhappy marriages who escape the atmosphere at home and spend an evening there, sometimes part of the night. The countess keeps them in order. Everyone tries to behave like it's high society. But they'll whine pitifully if they have to settle a debt of thirty or forty francs . . .'

'Has Le Cloaguen ever set foot inside the club?'

'He's not on the list.'

'What about his wife? . . . Or daughter?'

'I thought of that. No one ever heard of them . . .'

'How about Mademoiselle Jeanne?'

'Got something there . . . When I showed the countess her photo, I got the impression that she batted an eyelid. She stared at it hard, too hard, then she asked in a voice that sounded a bit strained: "Who is this person?"'

The waiter in the Brasserie Dauphine, who knows the offices of the Police Judiciaire as well as the tables in his bar, has put the two beers on the desk. Maigret downs the first in one. The other is already in his hand. He catches Lucas's eye and mutters:

'Sorry. Hope you don't mind . . .'

His thirst is too great. It's too bad for Lucas, who has had plenty of opportunity to quench his thirst on the way here!

'I'm wondering . . .'

Noon strikes. Hundreds of thousands of Parisians will

be making the most of the weekend and taking themselves off to the seaside or the country.

'Hello? . . . Switchboard? . . . Get my wife on the line . . .'

The second glass is almost empty. Both Maigret's pipes on the desk are hot.

'Madame Maigret? Is that you? . . . What? . . . No, I'm not ringing to say I won't be home for lunch . . . The very opposite . . . I'll be there in . . . say an hour . . . Meanwhile, pack the tan case . . . Yes, the tan one . . . We're going to spend the weekend by the river . . . At Morsang . . . Yes . . . See you soon . . .'

'What am I supposed to be doing?' asks Lucas, who already knows that he won't be spending the weekend in the country.

Maigret, pencil in hand, writes a list of lines of inquiry for everyone to follow up. Rue Coulaincourt . . . The green convertible . . . Question all the shopkeepers and bistro staff . . . Boulevard des Batignolles . . . Too bad if nothing comes of it all, but it's vital for Le Cloaguen to be closely tailed . . . Why not send a man to watch Place des Vosges? . . . Yes . . . A man posted near the fountain, to see if certain persons might want to take a look round Mascouvin's cheerless apartment.

Forgotten anything? Orders for the house switchboard. Make a record of all the countess's phone calls. Also Le Cloaguen's. You never know.

As for the man with the two gold teeth, Vice and the Gambling Squad are already looking after him and also tomorrow, on race-courses . . .

'See you Monday, Lucas.'

'Have a good time, sir.'

Maigret has already got his hat on when he stops.

'By the way, there's this girl, a Mademoiselle Berthe . . . Maybe it's nothing . . . But never mind . . . On Monday I'll want to know what she does between now and then . . .'

'Pretty is she, sir?'

'A peach . . . And maybe a peach with a heart . . .'

Finally, shaking hands on the way, Maigret walks down the dusty stairs of the Police Judiciaire.

4. Monsieur Blaise Catches Two Pike

There are days which, though you don't know why, sum up a season, a phase of your life, a whole gamut of sensations. That Saturday night at Morsang and the Sunday that followed were for Maigret the quintessence of summers spent by the river, the ease of life and the simple, sweet pleasures.

The lanterns under the trees which did not have to be lit until the end of dinner; the leaves which turned a sumptuous dark green, the green of old tapestries; the whitish mist which rose off the moving surface of the Seine; the sound of laughter from the small restaurant tables and the dreamy voices of loving couples . . .

The Maigrets were in bed when someone had brought a gramophone out on to the hotel terrace, and for some considerable time they had heard the sounds of soft, easy music and the crunch of gravel under the feet of dancers.

Did the inspector really get any sleep that night? The annex of the Beau Pigeon, where the bedrooms were located, resembled a ship, with its exterior iron stairs and the balcony running along the entire length of the first floor. The rooms were small, like cabins, with whitewashed walls, an iron bed, bathroom and a deal hanging closet behind a cretonne curtain . . . That night everyone slept with their doors and windows open to the August night . . .

'Have you got enough room?' breathed Madame Maigret, hugging the wall.

Of course he didn't! The bed was far too small for two people. Maigret was beginning to drop off when a sound percolated into his slumber: first, a splash of oars around three o'clock, a rowing-boat being untied; he knew it was Isidore, the inn's general handyman, who was going out to lift the eel-pots.

Later, a baby crying. Among the people staying there some young families, in the majority, two dentists, an insurance inspector, some haute couture salesgirls . . . and all of them were happy and easy-going.

'Where have you got to, Maigret?'

In the half-light, Madame Maigret made out her husband, braces dangling from his waistband, leaning with his elbows on the taffrail. A fine curl of blue smoke rose from his pipe.

'Tomorrow you'll only want to have a nap after lunch . . .'

Disjointed thoughts . . . Mademoiselle Jeanne often came to the Beau Pigeon . . . She danced too . . . The other hotel guests did not know what she did for a living and, among other things, she would go out for a row on the river with Madame Rialand, the dentist's wife . . .

A train on the far side of the Seine, a boat returning noiselessly, the dark shape of Isidore, tall, thin, leather leggings, hunting jacket, drooping moustache . . . He made for the kitchen, where he would light the lamp and set down a bucket full of water containing live gudgeon and roach . . .

People were waking up here and there. An angler came

out of his room on the ground floor, filling his first pipe of the day, and went to get his fishing tackle from a shed.

Another man . . . The pair of them shook hands . . . Isidore took something, a longish bundle, from the locker of his boat, climbed aboard another boat, newly painted a delicate green, and slipped the bundle into its locker . . .

It was as if there was something almost ritualistic about all this activity, as though every fine Sunday brought out the same anglers, the same couples, the same early-morning starts . . .

Isidore was now wiping the dew off the dinghy and fetching fishing lines and rods, which he arranged care-fully, while an agreeable smell of coffee drifted up from the kitchen, where a maid had come down, hair uncombed, only half-dressed under her apron.

What's this? Monsieur Blaise had been occupying the room next to Maigret's. He emerged now, muttered a shy 'good morning' and went down the metal stairs. One of the establishment's most loyal customers, according to Madame Roy. A quiet, mild-mannered, middle-aged man, always extremely well turned out.

In the kitchen, his lunch-hamper was being got ready: a half chicken, a half bottle of burgundy, cheese, fruit and a bottle of mineral water. Isidore escorted him to his boat, the stern of which was fitted with an outboard motor with a cord-pull start.

The air was growing lighter. Imperceptibly, other anglers, probably from the village on the opposite bank, had found spots among the trees lining the river. The motor was run-ning. Seated by himself in the stern, Monsieur Blaise, with a cigarette between his lips, moved upstream, letting out a pike line with a metal lure which trailed in the wake of the boat.

'Sleep well?'

'And you?'

The pace of things was quickening. People came and went in their pyjamas, in dressing gowns, both maids now fully dressed went into the rooms bearing breakfast trays.

'Are you there, Maigret? . . . What are you doing?'

Nothing . . . Mademoiselle Jeanne . . . Odd that Madame Roy should have gone to see her with the tench just moments after the murder had been committed . . . Oddest of all, surely, is the presence, in the kitchen, behind a door of which the key has not been found, of old Le Cloaguen, who claims he doesn't know anything . . .

Children are eating their breakfasts at small tables under the trees. Couples wearing very little carry glossy-hulled canoes, and a young man in thick glasses hoists the sail of a very small royal-blue boat.

'Aren't you going fishing?'

No! Maigret is going to do nothing. It's after nine when he decides to shave and finish getting dressed. He breakfasts on sausage and a half-litre of white wine. As far as the eye can see, the Seine is being churned up by boats, single-seater canoes and miniature yachts, and anglers sit without moving every fifty or sixty metres without fail.

The hours glide by as gently as the water in the river. Places for lunch are already being laid, and a few cars arrive from Paris and overflow the courtyard of the inn. Madame Maigret who can never sit still doing nothing, has brought her needlework. On principle, since after all they are in the country, she is sitting on the grass, although there are plenty of chairs all around her.

The canoes come in one after the other, a few of the anglers too, but others who are much keener, like Monsieur Blaise, took their lunch with them when they left.

Monsieur Blaise must have gone a fair way up the reach, towards Seine-Port, for his boat has not been seen all morning. Still, a wide swathe of the opposite bank after the bend in the river has been overrun by reeds, and this lends the vista a deceptively exotic look, like an aquatic jungle where young lovers in canoes deliberately arrange to get lost.

Isidore has been looking after everything, racking wine, going to Corbeil in the car to pick up the meat, repairing a boat which has sprung a leak . . .

Three o'clock. From time to time Madame Maigret casts a protective glance at her husband, who has fallen asleep in a chair, and it would not take much for her to tell the people round about to be quiet.

He is not sleeping that deeply because he has heard the phone ring. He looks at his watch, stands up and reaches the house just as a maid appears at the door and calls: 'Phone for Monsieur Maigret!'

It is Lucas. Maigret had told him to watch the house on Boulevard des Batignolles and to phone him at about three.

'That you, sir?'

Hm. There's a contrite tone in the sergeant's voice.

'There's been a bit of a hitch, but I swear that I couldn't

have been more careful . . . First thing this morning I noticed that a curtain at one of the windows was moving. But there was no way I could be recognized because I was disguised as a tramp and . . .'

'Moron!'

'What? . . . I didn't catch . . .'

Everyone in the Police Judiciaire knows that Maigret hates disguises. But there was no way of preventing Lucas, who loves dressing up, from getting into character.

'To cut a long story short, about eleven this morning . . .'

'Who came out?'

'The wife . . . She didn't even look round her. She headed off towards Place Clichy and there got the Métro . . . I was right behind her and I swear . . .'

'Where did she lose you?'

'How did you know? She got off at Saint-Jacques underground station . . . You know where I mean? . . . The boulevard was completely deserted. Opposite the station exit, there was a taxi, just one. She got into it, behaving normally, and then it drove off. I spent ten minutes trying to find another one . . .'

'You don't say.'

'I got the taxi's number . . . Well, sir, turns out it's false. There is no such number plate in records . . . I went back to Boulevard des Batignolles after I got changed . . .'

'I assume that you're back now as Lucas?'

'Yes . . . The concierge says Madame Le Cloaguen hasn't come back. The old man must be locked up in his room because he hasn't gone out. Nor has the daughter . . .'

An empty Paris, with avenues and streets that look

wider and airier . . . The choice of Boulevard Saint-Jacques, one of the furthest from central Paris . . .

Maigret is suddenly sobered.

'Well, there we are . . .' he growled.

'What do I do now?'

'You wait . . . Phone me when she gets back . . . By the way . . . Listen . . . Be sure and get a good look at her shoes. I'd be interested to know if they've got dust on them . . .'

'Understood, sir . . .'

Wrong. Lucas has not understood. The thought that has only just crossed Maigret's mind is still unformed . . .

He steps out of the phone booth, prowls briefly around the inn, smiles at Madame Roy, who smiled at him first. But it's a sombre smile.

'When I think of that poor woman, inspector . . .'

'Was she particularly friendly with any of your customers?'

'No . . . I can't think . . . She was quite a shy person. This is her table, here. I feel like crying every time I look in this direction . . . She loved children. That's why she was so often with Madame Rialand, the dentist's wife, who's got two, Monique and Jean-Claude . . .'

Maigret stands in the doorway. His face is now not quite as relaxed as it usually is on sunny Sundays. One detail puzzles, bothers him. The business of the solitary taxi outside the Saint-Jacques Métro station. It's so obvious! Whoever pulled that fast one on Lucas is not a child – and no amateur either!

Has the wiry, nervous Madame Le Cloaguen gone for good? The inspector is convinced she hasn't. In that case, why did she feel the need to be free of surveillance for a few hours? Was it to meet someone? To move some papers to a safe place? To . . .

Look! The inspector recognizes a persistent thrum in the distance. It's the outboard motor on Monsieur Blaise's boat. Soon in the dappled sunlight its very raised bow becomes visible and in it the calm, collected figure of the fisherman as he steers an elegant curve before making for the floating landing stage and cutting the engine.

Two or three strollers gather round, as always happens when a fisherman ties up. Isidore arrives at a run.

'Catch anything, Monsieur Blaise?'

Almost casually and with a practised air of a man used to catching fish, Monsieur Blaise says:

'Couple of pike . . . Not too bad . . .'

He opens the boat's locker revealing a cloth on which the two pike are wrapped in leaves to keep them fresh.

Monsieur Blaise has caught Maigret's eye and, as he had that morning, gives him a guarded nod. When people are staying at the same inn, in the country . . .

He gets out of the boat and walks slowly up to his room. Maigret has made sure of getting a good look at his shoes, which are clean, with no dust on them.

Isidore who has already started putting the fishing tackle away, looks up because Maigret, like some credulous Parisian townie, is talking to him.

'Did he catch them with a trail net from the stern?'

'Don't think so. I'd put live bait in the boat. When the drag doesn't net anything, Monsieur Blaise, who knows all the best spots, will use a line with live bait. He doesn't often come back empty-handed . . .'

'May I . . . ?'

As Maigret gets into the boat, he almost upsets it. He bends down and picks up one of the pike.

'A beauty, it really is . . .'

'Middling size. Six or seven pounder . . .'

But suddenly Isidore gives the inspector a sharper look and takes both fish from him.

'If you don't mind . . . I'll have to wrap them for him. He's bound to want to take them back to Paris . . .'

Isidore goes off to the kitchen.

'What are you doing, Maigret?' asks Madame Maigret placidly.

Nothing . . . He's doing nothing . . . He's waiting for something . . . He pretends to be fascinated by the manoeuvres of a sailing boat which is trying unsuccessfully to travel upstream when there is no breeze to fill its sail.

That's it! . . . His heart misses a beat! . . . The light of triumph in his eye . . . Because, say what you like, it's always very gratifying . . . Maigret knew it would happen . . . He was certain of it . . . And yet all he had to go on were hunches, very fine details . . .

It was a miracle that these top rooms had been too hot; a miracle that he had felt the charm of an August night and that with his braces hanging down his sides he should have been up to observe the sunrise.

Isidore's actions that morning, in the gloom . . . Maigret clearly saw him take something from his boat, a longish bundle, and put it in the locker of Monsieur Blaise's boat. Now, it couldn't have been the live bait. The

59

live bait was in a square metal container, with a lid riddled with holes. The inspector did not think it important at the time . . .

It was Lucas's phone call that started it off . . .

Then the two pike . . . He's had a pretty good look at them . . . Maigret had done some fishing in his day and though he might not have caught too many fish, at least he knew a thing or two about the technique . . .

The most difficult job is getting the hook out of a pike, the most voracious of all river fish. It's so difficult that sometimes you have to cut its belly open.

Neither of the pike caught by Monsieur Blaise has a wound or even a scratch on it!

And Isidore was out fishing with a net for a large part of the night . . .

What happens now is the logical consequence of the way Isidore looked at the inspector. After passing through the kitchen, Isidore has walked all round the buildings, climbed up to the first floor of the annex and has gone almost furtively into Monsieur Blaise's room.

To keep him up to date!

Kindly Madame Maigret, who thinks that her husband is getting bored, murmurs:

'You ought to have brought a book . . . Seeing that for once you're taking time off . . .'

Ah! there's no doubt about it . . . He is being watched from up there . . . Isidore comes down . . . He moves like a cat or a poacher . . .

'Aren't you tired yet with standing all this time? . . .'

Monsieur Blaise's window is open. The man inside is

visible; he has got changed and is just finishing putting on his town clothes.

'Tell me, Madame Roy . . .'

'I'm listening, inspector . . .'

A few questions asked in a matter-of-fact voice.

Yes, Monsieur Blaise gets here by the Saturday evening train, and usually goes back on Sunday by the six o'clock. It'll soon be time for him to go across the river by the dam.

No, he never comes by car.

Women? . . . The very idea! The thought has never entered her head. He doesn't bother with women. Never once has he come to the Beau Pigeon with anyone.

What? In the villas across the river? She's never thought of that either. It's out of the question, he's out fishing all day. Anyway, the one or two villas you can see all belong to well-heeled families from Paris. There's the Mallets, who are in river transport – their offices are on Quai Voltaire . . . Also the Duroys, an old couple who . . .

'Sh! . . . He's coming . . .'

Monsieur Blaise, who must be Maigret's age, looks a lot younger. He gives the impression that he looks after his appearance and leads an untroubled existence.

'How are we, Madame Roy? . . .'

'And yourself, Monsieur Blaise? . . . I hear you've had a good day's fishing? . . .'

'Not bad.'

She adds teasingly, with even a hint of familiarity:

'And did you sleep well? . . . Admit it: you can't just fish from dawn to dusk and when your boat is moored in the reeds . . .'

'I never sleep during the day,' he replies, suddenly curt.

'Oh, there's no harm in it. Why only just now, Monsieur Maigret . . .'

A quick – too quick – instinctive glance from Monsieur Blaise. Was he really unaware of the identity of the inspector?

The phone rings. Maigret picks up the receiver. He is not surprised to hear Lucas's voice.

'She's back, sir . . . No, not in a taxi . . . Turned up on foot, from the direction of Rue d'Amsterdam . . .'

'What about her shoes?'

'You were right . . . Then almost as soon as she got back, the old man came out . . . In no hurry . . . Went for his usual walk . . . I've got a uniformed man watching while I'm phoning . . . What do I do now? . . .'

It is Lucas's favourite question. Maigret gives him detailed instructions.

'Ah! . . . Monsieur Blaise has gone . . .' he says, emerging from the phone booth.

He looks out and in the distance sees the ferryman's boat but not his man.

'Tell me, Madame Roy, how come he hasn't crossed the river?'

'You mean Monsieur Blaise? . . . Ah, yes! . . . The moment you were called to the phone, there were some guests leaving by car . . .'

'Did he know these people?'

'No . . . I know because he approached them, very apologetic, asked if they could take him as far as Corbeil, because he was afraid of missing his train . . .'

'Did he take his pike with him?'

'Oh yes! . . . He had his bundle under his arm . . .'

'Of course, I don't suppose you remember the number of the car?'

She suddenly takes fright.

'Whatever are you thinking, inspector? A man like Monsieur Blaise! He's the one I always ask for advice about what I should do about investing my money . . . He keeps up to date with the Stock Exchange . . .'

'Do you know his address in Paris?'

'It must be in the hotel register . . . Just a moment . . . But I'm wondering . . . Yes, really wondering what makes you think . . .'

'I don't think anything, Madame Roy . . . Let's see . . . Blaise . . . B . . . Blochet, Bardamont . . . Blaise . . . Profession: none . . . 25, Notre Dame-de-Lorette . . .'

Madame Roy gives a nervous laugh.

'I can't think that . . . I don't know what you . . . Well, they do say policemen have a habit of suspecting everybody of something . . .'

'Do you mind if I use your phone again?'

'Corbeil: Railways Police inspector. No, the train for Paris hasn't been through yet . . . Another couple of minutes. Description? . . . Right! . . . Call you back . . .'

'Police Judiciaire, Paris: 25, Rue Notre-Dame-de-Lorette . . . Who's on duty? . . . Dupré? . . . Dupré is fine, but tell him to try and look natural! . . .'

Madame Roy is busying about in her kitchen and she is cross.

'Could I have a small calvados, please?'

He waits for the phone to ring. He is not surprised to discover that no one answering to the description of Monsieur Blaise got on the Paris train at Corbeil station.

Two hours later, when everyone registered at the Beau Pigeon is sitting down to dinner and the visitors' cars are beginning to leave, Dupré is next to phone. Monsieur Blaise has not come home.

'Are we going to stay here another night?' asks Madame Maigret. 'It's such a narrow bed! . . . I don't mind for myself, but you hardly got a wink of sleep last night . . .'

That is of no importance. While Isidore is mooring the guests' boats, Maigret stands, inscrutable, by the water's edge.

'It's bizarre!' observes the inspector.

'What's bizarre?'

'This craze anglers have! . . . Don't think I didn't spot it! He doesn't want to look like a learner. Oh no! He's got his pride. So it was you who . . .'

Isidore hesitates a moment then makes up his mind and winks.

'For a good customer, you know, we can always . . .'

The gramophone. There are only three couples dancing under the trees on the terrace.

Phone. Dupré at last! It's eleven o'clock.

'Monsieur Blaise has just got home . . . What? . . . What do you mean, pike? . . . No, he didn't have any pike . . . What's all this about pike, sir? . . . Want me to stay? . . . Right! . . . That's fine! . . . I understand . . .'

Tens of thousands of Parisians are now getting home with a taste of country and sweat on their lips and flowers from field and woods filling their cars.

'That you, sir?'

Now it's Lucas's turn.

'Nothing to report . . . The old man got home at seven . . . No one's come out . . . They're probably all in bed now because there are no lights showing . . . Shall I hand over to Janvier? . . . Good night, sir . . . Thanks . . .'

It's a bit like the watchman's cry in times gone by: 'Midnight and all is well! . . .'

A final phone call from the inspector in charge of the Rue Coulaincourt police station.

'Nothing to report . . .'

But on this fine Sunday, something has happened for sure. As yet only a glimpse of distant eddies, of bubbles on the surface of the water that reveal the presence of fish which are disturbing the mud on the bottom.

'What if I asked if they have another room so that you could have the bed to yourself and sleep through?'

The moon rises. The gramophone falls silent, though one couple still makes the gravel crunch in the dark.

5. A Man Complains

That day, Maigret had almost reached the point of being ashamed of being a policeman. From time to time, just as an actor uses an exit from the stage to stand in the wings for a moment to wipe the sweat off and let his features and muscles relax, he would step into the office next door, where Lucas was scarcely less proud of himself than he was.

'Anything?' was the question in the sergeant's eyes.

Nothing. Maigret took a sip of beer and stood at the open window, morose, care-worn and feeling sick to the stomach.

'What is *she* playing at?'

'This is the third time she's been on at the duty officer at the desk insisting on speaking to you. Last time, she demanded to see the commissioner of the Police Judiciaire.'

Actually, it lent some light relief to the situation . . . At two o'clock, the time he had notified Octave Le Cloaguen to come to see him in his office, the inspector had glanced out of his window and seen a taxi draw up outside on Quai des Orfèvres. Out of it got the scrawny figure of Madame Le Cloaguen. The vehicle remained at the kerb. Maigret had smiled and given an order to an officer.

And that is where the whole episode had turned farcical.

'Do you have an appointment?' the clerk asked solemnly. 'Are you Octave Le Cloaguen? . . .'

'I would like to see the detective chief inspector . . . I shall explain to him . . .'

She was shown into the famous glazed waiting room where detainees (the word is chosen advisedly) under the eye, calm or sardonic, of passing inspectors had a vague feeling that they were being caged, like animals.

While she was kept waiting, an inspector went out to fetch Le Cloaguen, who was sitting in the taxi.

'Was it my wife who said I should go up?'

'No, the detective chief inspector.'

'Where is my wife?'

It was now three hours that the old man in the greenish overcoat had been in Maigret's office, sitting on the same chair, facing the open window.

Each time Maigret came back from brief breaks next door with Lucas, the moment he crossed the threshold he was confronted by the pale stare of Le Cloaguen, the look of a dog which knows it has little to expect from man but is equally certain that it cannot escape his power.

Yes, that was exactly what that expression signified. Resignation so utter that it was painful to see, because it took little imagination to know that to sink that low the old man must have suffered greatly.

Three or four times he had asked the same thing:

'Where is Madame Le Cloaguen?'

'She's waiting for you . . .'

The answer did not reassure him. He knew his impatient, imperious wife only too well, and he could imagine that she would not be sitting demurely in a waiting room.

In the time-honoured way, Maigret had begun with the

'soft' routine: some pretty good-natured, friendly questions asked as if no particular importance was being attached to them, and making it seem as if the interview was just a formality.

'The other day I forgot to clear up one point . . . You said that when there was that special knock on Mademoiselle Jeanne's door, she was in the middle of telling your fortune with cards. Is that right?'

Le Cloaguen listened without answering, giving the impression he did not understand.

'Mademoiselle Jeanne pushed you into a room and locked the door behind you. Now, what I'd like to know is whether the cards stayed on the table or whether she picked them up . . . Take your time . . . Collect your thoughts . . . God knows why, but the examining magistrate attaches an importance to this question which in my view is excessive . . .'

Le Cloaguen does not move. He sighs, with his hands resting on his knees, those hands which again draw Maigret's attention as they had in the taxi.

'Try and picture the scene . . . It's hot . . . The window that leads out on to the balcony is open . . . Everything is light and airy around you, and the cards with their various colours are spread out on the marble top of the Louis XV table . . .'

The expression in the old man's eyes seems to be saying: 'You don't understand, do you, what I'm going through, that you are tormenting a defenceless old man?'

Maigret looks away, feeling ashamed, then says in his kindly voice:

'Please answer the question . . . This is not an official interview, because what you say is not being written down . . . The cards remained on the table, didn't they?'

'Yes . . .'

'Are you sure?'

'Yes . . .'

'It was a full reading that Mademoiselle Jeanne was doing for you?'

'Yes . . .'

At this, Maigret gets up, goes to the door, calls in Lucas and says in a scathing voice:

'Honestly, sergeant . . . I can tell you now: your information is incorrect, because I really don't think Monsieur Le Cloaguen has come here to tell me lies . . .'

Well, well! As one former interior minister famously said, you don't run a police force by employing choirboys. Do murderers have scruples?

'You stated clearly, sergeant, did you not, that Mademoiselle Jeanne did not tell fortunes with cards, and that there wasn't even a pack of cards in the whole place? . . .'

'That's right. All the witness statements are in agreement on that point. Mademoiselle Jeanne was not a fortune-teller who read cards but an extra-lucid clairvoyant who put herself in trances using a crystal ball like they do in the Orient . . .'

'Oh dear, Monsieur Le Cloaguen! . . . I expect you didn't hear my question properly a few moments ago, or did you answer without thinking? There weren't any cards on the table, were there?'

Beads of sweat appear on his forehead, and the veins stand out.

'I don't know . . .' he mutters.

'Lucas, you can go! . . . Monsieur Le Cloaguen, I'm sorry to bring up a delicate matter . . . I think I can guess . . . It's clear, in fact it's patently obvious, that you are not very happy at home . . . In your position you, like many men of your age, looked for consolation elsewhere, friendship, affection, a little feminine warmth. I knew from the start that you weren't the sort of man who has his fortune told. If you were in Rue Coulaincourt, if your lady friend hid you in her kitchen, it was because you weren't there as a client . . .'

The old man does not dare say yes and he does not dare say no. What new surprise will the inspector spring on him when he returns from the office next door after gathering his strength and lights a fresh pipe with such exasperating slowness?

'You're the only one who can help us. We know very little about the victim. All we know is that when she came to Paris she worked first as a seamstress then as a model. Later she opened a modest dressmaker's shop in Rue Saint-Georges called Chez Jeanne, and the name Jeanne stuck to her. The business did not make money, and she moved to Rue Coulaincourt . . . What contacts did she have? Who were her friends? It's vital that we establish facts like that . . .'

'I don't know anything . . .'

'Come now! I can understand that you wish to be discreet. But don't forget that our only concern is to punish the man who murdered your friend.'

It's enough to try the patience of a saint. And now the old man has started crying, sobbing bitterly, silently, without stirring, without wiping his eyes, without removing those gnarled hands from his knees! To hide his frustration, Maigret is obliged to turn his back on him and stare out of the window at a convoy of passing barges . . .

'None of this concerns your wife or anybody else . . . I'd even understand, since you are a wealthy man, if you'd given financial help to a young woman who needed money. Because it's obvious someone was helping her. She didn't make enough out of her men and women customers to cover her expenses, because, though she didn't live a life of luxury, she was comfortable . . . You have an income of 200,000 francs . . .'

The charade continues. Maigret shuffles the papers scattered over his desk.

'One of my men went the extra mile and looked into your financial situation . . . It's quite interesting! What we've found is all very much to your credit. Thirty years ago you worked as a doctor on a ship belonging to the Far Eastern line . . . An ultra-rich Argentinian beef baron was travelling with his daughter . . . There was an outbreak of yellow fever . . .'

Maigret continues to pretend to be looking through his papers . . .

'It appears that you were brilliant. Thanks to you, there was no panic on board. Moreover, you saved the girl's life . . . On the other hand, you went down with the fever yourself and when the ship reached port you had to be disembarked. At that point, the grateful Argentinian decided to settle on you an annual sum of 200,000 francs, for life . . . I congratulate you, Monsieur Le Cloaguen.

When you got back to France, you married the girl you were engaged to. You never went to sea again. You settled at Saint-Raphaël, where you lived happily for many years . . . Unfortunately, age made your wife avaricious and brought out the domineering streak in her character . . . In Paris your life changed . . .'

Surely the old man must be wondering how long this torture is going to last. Could it be about to end at any moment? Maigret gets to his feet and starts walking towards the door, smiling, like a man whose job is almost done, but suddenly changes his mind and finds another question to ask – just a small one, hardly a question at all.

'By the way, when you had your accident . . . It did happen at Saint-Raphaël, didn't it? Just before you left for Paris? . . . You were chopping firewood. You liked doing it yourself, because in those days you had just two maids . . . Caught yourself with the axe. Ended up, as it happened, with you losing the top joint of the index finger on your right hand . . . You must find it rather a handicap . . . I have no more questions for you, Monsieur Le Cloaguen . . .'

So it really is all over . . . But the man must have fathomed Maigret's method, for he doesn't get up yet; only his eyes are asking if he is really free to go.

'One of your friends was talking to me about you yesterday . . . Hang on! . . . I must have a photo of him somewhere in my drawer . . .'

It is a photograph of Monsieur Blaise which was taken as he walked along one of the main boulevards.

'Let's see . . . what was his name again? . . . You can probably remember . . . He told me . . .'

A bad move. Le Cloaguen looks at the photo without reacting ... If anything he seems relieved, as if he had been expecting something else ...

'Doesn't the picture remind you of anybody? ... Still, it's probably a long time since you lost sight of each other? ... It doesn't matter ...'

Maigret goes next door, where Lucas gives him a wink.

'I'd say it's only a matter of minutes before his wife makes a real scene. She refuses to stay put. She keeps bothering the desk officer every five minutes. She yells. She demands to see the commissioner. She's threatening to go to the newspapers and bring all her high-placed contacts into it ...'

It's been three hours since she was told to wait, three hours that the old man has been facing the ordeal of being alone with Maigret. But Maigret won't give way. This man makes him uneasy. He senses a mystery, and it irritates him. Yet at the same time he cannot stop feeling an odd kind of sympathy which is not just pity.

The 'singing session' goes on, 'softer' than ever. Maigret puts on a graver, embarrassed expression.

'Well now, there's something else which isn't going to make things any simpler. The examining magistrate has phoned to say that a new witness has come forward. It's a man who lives just opposite 67A, Rue Coulaincourt. He claims that last Friday, a few minutes after five, he saw you throwing a key out of the window ... The key has been found ...'

'I don't care ...' mutters Le Cloaguen.

'But his statement makes your position worse and ...'

Maigret places a key on his desk.

'You know very well, inspector, that it's not true,' murmurs the old man with disarming meekness.

'Listen, Monsieur Le Cloaguen . . . Why don't you admit that the life you lead is, to put it mildly, ambiguous? You are rich, intelligent. You were an exceptional ship's doctor and a man of courage, as your service record shows. And then all of a sudden you start living like a miserable wretch, at home you are locked up as if you're in the way and outside you spend each and every day wandering the streets and walking by the river. What happened to bring about such a change? Why did you leave Saint-Raphaël and settle in Paris? . . . Why? . . .'

Le Cloaguen looks up. His pale eyes are tragic in their frankness and he murmurs:

'You know I'm not right in the head . . .'

'What you mean is that certain people, your wife and perhaps your daughter, keep trying to convince you that you're mad? . . .'

He shakes his head and repeats flatly, stubbornly:

'No, I am mad . . .'

'Think about the seriousness of what you're saying. If you really are mad, which I don't believe, there is nothing to say that you are not the man who murdered Mademoiselle Jeanne . . . No one can anticipate what a madman will do . . . You were in her flat . . . The idea of killing her enters your head . . . You acted on the idea, then you become lucid again. You are frightened by the consequences of what you've done and to deflect suspicion or because you hear someone coming up the stairs, you shut yourself inside the kitchen and throw the key out of the window . . .'

No reply.

'Is that how it happened?'

Maigret is almost afraid to hear a yes, even though it would bring the entire investigation to a close. What he gets is a very different result. It has taken three hours to extract a statement which casts a faint glimmer of light on . . .

'I'm mad all right, but I didn't kill Jeanne . . .'

'You called her Jeanne . . . I take it then that you admit that you were very close to her? . . . Tell me exactly what she meant to you . . . Don't feel embarrassed . . . We're used to hearing all kinds of things here . . .'

'I have nothing to say . . . I am very, *very* tired . . .'

Then he adds, shamefaced and shy:

'I'm thirsty . . .'

At this, Maigret goes next door again, returns with a large glass of beer; the old man's face goes down to the beer, and the level drops as his Adam's apple moves up and down.

'Where did your wife go on Sunday between eleven and four?'

'I didn't even know she'd gone out.'

'Were you locked up in your room?'

No reply. The old man stares at the floor. Maigret would give his right arm for one moment of plain candour. Of all the men he's ever interviewed – and quite a few have passed through this office on Quai des Orfèvres! – never before when confronted by any man has he felt he was dealing with such an enigma. The inspector feels frustrated and bored at the same time. There are moments when his hackles rise and he feels he could . . .

'Listen, Le Cloaguen, you can't tell me you don't know anything, not even why they lock you up like a dog with the mange . . .'

'It's because I'm mad . . .'

'Mad people don't know they're mad.'

'But I am mad . . . I never killed anyone, inspector . . . I haven't done anything wrong . . . I swear you're wide of the mark to . . .'

'In that case why don't you talk, for God's sake?'

'What do you want me to say?'

Either he's the stupidest man on earth or else . . .

'Look at me, in the eye . . . On my desk there's an arrest warrant made out in your name . . . If your answers are not satisfactory I can arrange for you to spend tonight here, in the cells . . .'

Whereupon the most unexpected thing happens. Instead of being frightened, the old man looks reassured, content. It's as if the prospect of going to jail is a pleasant proposition.

Could it be that the thought of escaping the tyranny of both women . . .

'Why do you let them order you around without complaining? . . . Just between the two of us men . . . All your neighbours talk about you. Some scoff, others feel sorry for you . . .'

'My wife looks after me . . .'

'What, by letting you go out winter and summer in an

old overcoat a tramp wouldn't be seen dead in? By refusing to give you money to buy tobacco? Yesterday, an inspector saw you picking up a cigarette end in the street as if you were down and out . . . You, with an income of 200,000 francs a year! . . .'

No reply. Maigret loses his temper:

'You are locked up in the darkest, shabbiest room on the apartment. They hide you from visitors as if you were some undesirable or repulsive creature . . .'

'I tell you she really looks after me . . .'

'What you mean is that your wife and daughter don't let you die! And you know exactly why that is. When your Argentinian beef baron was so grateful that he settled an income on you, could it be by chance that he drew up the papers in such a way that on your death your heirs and assigns wouldn't get another penny? The pension of 200,000 francs is paid to you personally . . . Isn't it true, Monsieur Le Cloaguen, that you know damn well why you are being, in your own words, taken good care of ? . . .'

Or is it possible that the man really is a saint?

'I swear, inspector . . .'

'That's enough! Carry on like this and you'll make me really angry! Listen, I haven't arrested you yet. I hope that you will reflect, that you will see that your best course would be to tell me everything . . . Lucas! . . . Lucas! . . .'

Lucas steps into the office, notes that his chief is sweating profusely and that he is barely containing his anger.

'Bring Madame Le Cloaguen here . . .'

The old man's hands begin to shake, his forehead again

breaks out in that same ugly sweat of fear. Could it be that they do actually beat him?

'Come in, madame! . . . Be quiet! . . . I would ask you not to speak . . . I realize that you feel angry about having been kept waiting for hours, but you only have yourself to blame . . . Be quiet! . . . It was your husband I sent for, not you. He's quite old enough to be able to come to Quai des Orfèvres by himself, and if it happens again you will not be allowed into the building . . . I return him to you. I don't know yet if I shall need to take further action against him. But it is at least likely that he will be examined by doctors, who will be able to tell us if he really is mad or not . . . You may go . . . I am asking you to leave, is that clear? . . . As you wish! You can complain to whoever you like . . . Goodbye, madame . . .'

Phew! . . . At last the door has closed. Lucas, greatly impressed, eyes his chief, who wipes his face, calms down slowly and even raises a smile.

'Well?'

'Nothing, Lucas . . . Absolutely zero . . . It's just that I can't stand the sight of that woman . . . I'd give anything for it to be her, instead of her husband, who was found in the kitchen of the flat in Rue Coulaincourt . . .'

Lucas smiles. Never before has he seen Maigret get so riled.

'Makes you think . . .' continues the inspector, suddenly pensive.

He stands as if suspended in time, his eyes fixed on the light-filled river scene and the variegated bustle on the Pont Saint-Michel.

'Makes you think of what? . . .'

'Oh, nothing . . . We need to know where that woman was on Friday afternoon. And know beyond doubt . . . You can look after that . . .'

'Why didn't you question her about what she did on Sunday?'

'Never you mind!'

Because he is convinced that she was expecting him to ask, that she had her answer all ready and that what ruffles her feathers, worries her and makes her see red is the fact that she wasn't asked any questions at all. Even now, in the taxi taking her home, she must be tormented by all kinds of fears.

'So you think . . .'

'I don't think anything . . . Who knows? . . . I might just take a trip down to Saint-Raphaël . . . And what about our other freak, the idiot Mascouvin? . . . Did you phone the Hôtel-Dieu?'

'His condition is satisfactory. His sister went to visit him, and he didn't recognize her. Give it another couple of days . . .'

'What about the man in the green convertible?'

'Nothing . . . He's probably changed his car . . . We are on to the twentieth green convertible, and the girl from the dairy hasn't recognized any of them . . .'

There is a knock at the door. It's the clerk.

'The commissioner wants to see you, sir.'

Maigret and Lucas exchange looks. It's never a good sign in the middle of an investigation. It means that there's something wrong, a hitch, complaints, God knows what.

Maigret is in no mood to accept a reprimand or even advice. Even the way he clamps the stem of his pipe between his teeth says a great deal about his intentions.

He opens the baize door.

'You sent for me?'

Without saying a word, the commissioner holds out a letter sent by pneumatic post which has just come. His attitude is neither one thing nor another, perhaps not best pleased or maybe just ironic. Maigret reads:

Dear commissioner.

I have the honour and advantage of bringing to your attention certain facts which, if they cannot be explained by any of your officers, would provide me with ample grounds to lodge a formal complaint.

On my return on Sunday last from my regular visit to Morsang-sur-Seine, I was told by my concierge that an individual, describing himself as a police inspector, had walked into her lodge a little earlier and had spent a considerable time asking questions about me, my means and my habits.

My concierge omitted to require this person to show any credentials. I have every reason to believe that he was a bogus policeman.

Indeed, by looking out at my surroundings through my window, I was able to catch sight of him watching me from a small café in Place Saint-Georges called the Vieux Pouilly.

I assume that, knowing I live alone and take all my meals in restaurants, he was only waiting for me to go out so that he could make a profitable visit to my apartment

I will not hide the fact that I play the stock market, an activity which is open to all French citizens, nor that I am in the habit of keeping large amounts of cash as well as share certificates at home.

I reported the facts enumerated above to my local police station and requested the protection of their officers. Shortly after this, I did observe a uniformed sergeant arrive in Rue Notre-Dame-de-Lorette.

The man who had been watching me spoke to him. They shook hands, and the sergeant walked off shrugging his shoulders.

The following morning, the watching man was still there. He was approached by a man of middle years, heavy-set with badly cut clothes, with whom he had a drink in the Vieux Pouilly . . .

The commissioner cannot resist smiling at Maigret's grim face, for it is patently obvious that the man referred to in the letter is the detective chief inspector himself.

I cannot help thinking that there is an organized gang which has designs on my money. The whole of Monday I was followed by men who seemed to operate in relays and were all fairly conspicuous.

Eventually when, as I do each week, I called in at Proud and Drouin, the agency which looks after all my investments, I discovered that the man with the heavy features and the pipe had been there inquiring if I was a client.

I would be most grateful if you would use every means

at your disposal to throw light on these facts and put an end
to a state of affairs which I regard as worrying.

Yours very sincerely,

Émile Blaise,

Registered Trader

'Well, Maigret?'

Already ready to explode when he walked into the commissioner's office, Maigret snorts menacingly, like a bear maddened beyond endurance.

'Yes, what do you make of this? Either this Monsieur Blaise is . . .'

At this, Maigret thunders:

'Monsieur Blaise? . . . Monsieur Blaise? . . . Monsieur Blaise is taking you for a ride, sir!'

'You too, I think . . .'

'Me too, yes . . .'

'Is it true you went to see Proud and Drouin?'

'Quite true. And I was damn well right! It would take too long to explain the ins and outs . . . You remember Mascouvin? The man who brought us the famous blotter? . . . Well, Mascouvin worked as a clerk at Proud and Drouin . . .'

'But who is this Monsieur Blaise?'

'Wait! Who discovered the body? A certain Madame Roy, landlady of the Beau Pigeon, at Morsang . . .'

'I still don't see . . .'

'Mademoiselle Jeanne used to go to Morsang often . . . Monsieur Blaise goes there every week and he catches pike which have already been caught once before . . .'

'Listen, Maigret. I'm starting to think . . .'

'And I think I'm beginning to understand . . . Mascouvin warns us about the murder before it's committed. Mademoiselle Jeanne is killed at the stated time. Madame Roy discovers her body a few minutes later. Monsieur Blaise is a client of Proud and Drouin and a client of Madame Roy. There's only Le Cloaguen . . .'

Maigret pauses for a moment to think.

'That's two connections already . . . Proud and Drouin and Morsang . . . I think that this evening I shall go for a bridge lesson . . .'

'Bridge lesson?'

'At the countess's club . . . A most distinguished lady, apparently, who has come down in the world and now pays her way by issuing invitations to people who are lonely in Paris to come and play bridge in her rooms in Rue des Pyramides . . . For a consideration, of course . . . Now, suppose Monsieur Blaise is one of her clients . . .'

'Well?'

'Nothing, I realize that . . . It wouldn't prove a thing . . . But you'd have to admit it is a curious coincidence given the fact that Mascouvin, a clerk at Proud and Drouin, played bridge every evening at the countess's . . . If only that blasted Le Cloaguen . . .'

The commissioner shrugs his shoulders discreetly as if telling himself: 'This is no time to cross him . . .'

He holds out his hand.

'Good luck, Maigret . . . By the bye, about this Monsieur Blaise . . . Perhaps it might be an idea to go a little easier on him? . . . The man seems very prickly and very determined to make trouble for us . . . If the papers get hold of it or he manages to interest a member of parliament in his complaint . . .'

Naturally! Of course! We'll be careful, commissioner, but it's obvious you haven't just spent three hours alone with the captivating Le Cloaguen!

6. Maigret Discovers Picpus

Experts had pored over the enigma that was Picpus. The first thing millions of people opening their newspapers looked for in the large print of the headlines was that name. It caught on, it was on everyone's lips.

'Have you seen Picpus?'

'How is Picpus? How's Picpus getting on?'

Taxi-drivers had finally found a word for their cack-handed colleagues.

'Watch where you're going, Picpus!'

In the end, it was a fly, a common house-fly, which would ultimately lead to the elusive Picpus.

That morning, Maigret had got up later than usual, because he had stayed in the countess's club until two in the morning. The air still retained a little of the delicious coolness of night while the sun, gilding the houses, contained the promise of warm hours to come.

Maigret, who liked nothing better than not hurrying when Paris is waking up, had not gone straight from Boulevard Richard Lenoir to Quai des Orfèvres but had proceeded at a leisurely, gentlemanly pace along a round-about route which took in Place de la République.

The previous evening, he had played a clownish role in the club rooms in Rue des Pyramides. The moment he arrived, the countess, wearing a flowing gauzy gown and behaving more theatrically than a leading lady from the Comédie Française, had pounced.

'Not a word! . . . Come with me, *dear* inspector . . . If you only knew how *thrilled* I am to welcome such a famous man into my home . . .'

She dragged him into her sanctum. She talked and talked. She begged Maigret not to do anything that would cause a scandal in her club. She only admitted persons of good breeding, persons who occupied prominent positions in society . . .

'Only just now I was saying to the prince . . .'

Her hand, heavy with fake diamond rings, kept landing on the knee of the inspector, who looked glaucous-eyed at this frothing creature.

'So you would really like to spend an evening with us? . . . No, I do not know a Monsieur Blaise. The description you give of him does not put me in mind of any of our friends . . . For we are among friends here, are we not? . . . If everyone contributes to the expenses, as is only natural in times as difficult as these . . .'

Five minutes later, she was introducing Maigret – though his picture appeared frequently in the newspapers – as a retired colonel, and sat him down at her bridge table, the one reserved for beginners, where she could give him a lesson. She nevertheless found time to pass among the tables, whispering a warning to everyone present.

'He's the famous Detective Chief Inspector Maigret! Do try to appear as if you're not staring at him. He's come here incognito. He wants to ask my advice . . .'

Now, in the street, Maigret looked at the passers-by,

telling himself that Paris was full of thousands, millions of bizarre exhibits of that sort, of people living mysterious or amazing lives which are rarely uncovered and then only through some traumatic event.

He was approaching the Café des Sports in Place de la République. He went in, hesitating a moment between standing at the counter and finding a table inside, but then he thought he would sit where Joseph Mascouvin always sat. His mind was working mechanically. Picpus! Why Picpus, the name of a densely populated street in a poor part of Paris, a good distance away, near the Père-Lachaise cemetery?

'Waiter! . . . A beer . . .'

'Coming up, inspector . . . Just getting this cask on . . .'

Nestor, sleeves rolled up over his hairy forearms, wiped the counter and the pump, making them sparkle. The only other person in the bar was sitting in a corner, a girl up from the provinces. She had a suitcase and was most likely waiting for someone while she nursed a milky coffee.

'Well now, inspector, how's poor Monsieur Mascouvin getting on?'

Nestor leaned forward to set the glass of beer on the table. The inspector stared at his bald head, or more accurately watched the progress of a fly which settled on it without the waiter appearing to notice.

From the fly and the polished scalp, his eye travelled further, and suddenly Maigret grunted and almost shot to his feet like a shell from a cannon, much to the surprise of the waiter, who turned round quickly and, seeing no one, was even more baffled by the startling reflex of a policeman renowned for his placidity.

Maigret had just found Picpus! Picpus was there, on the wall, just opposite the table occupied each day by Joseph Mascouvin, the same table where the letter predicting the death of the clairvoyant had certainly been written.

Readers would have plenty to laugh about if the papers ever printed a picture of the famous Picpus!

Above the slot-machine hung a large publicity calendar, the kind some businesses still give away free to their customers.

Moving house?
For removals without tears,
Send for . . .

A print in brash, basic colours showed the cartoonish figure of a strong man in a striped sweater, with a flaming-red bushy beard, a crimson nose and Olympian muscles. This colossus was winking at the observer while juggling with a mirror-fronted wardrobe:

Send for Picpus!

The name, in bold type, caught the eye while underneath, in smaller letters could be read:

United Removals
101, Rue Picpus, Paris.

So there was no such person as Picpus. He was a grotesque caricature, an advertising slogan. One evening, a man had sat at this table to write a note. Then he had paused. How should he sign it? His eye had wandered around him and had come to rest on the calendar: Picpus!

Looking no further, the man – or woman – had written, perhaps with a crafty smile: *Signed, Picpus*.

Only one thing was certain: Maigret was not mistaken. He knew!

'Waiter! What do I owe you?'

Maigret wanted to take the calendar with him to hang in his own museum of crime, but decided to come back for it another day, when the investigation was over.

And why not, since it was only a few minutes' walk from Boulevard Bonne-Nouvelle, take the opportunity to call in at Proud and Drouin? On his first visit, he had not been able to meet the owners.

There were numerous offices in the building. The staircase needed sweeping. On the first-floor windows, half covered by green glass, were written the names of both associates.

'Monsieur Proud, please.'

'Are you wanting to speak to him personally?'

'Yes. It's personal.'

'Monsieur Proud died three years ago . . .'

Feeling thwarted, Maigret asked the man at the desk with the smug smile if he could see Monsieur Drouin. A few moments later, he was shown into the office of Monsieur Drouin, a man of fifty with suspicious eyes.

'Sit down, inspector. I found your card on my desk and I must admit . . .'

'I quite understand, Monsieur Drouin . . . But because there are some questions I have to ask you . . .'

'If this is about a client, I must warn you that we are bound by a duty of absolute confidentiality and, further, that we consider our hands to be tied by the requirements of professional discretion . . .'

'Will you tell me, Monsieur Drouin, if you thought Joseph Mascouvin was an honest employee?'

'If I hadn't, I would not have gone on employing him . . .'

'Did he have an important position in your organization?'

Monsieur Drouin rises, crosses to the door and opens it to make sure no one could hear them.

'Given the circumstances and the mystery surrounding the poor man's actions, I can tell you that I kept him on mainly out of charity . . .'

'Did he not give satisfaction?'

'Try to understand. I had no complaints from the point of view of his professional competence . . . On the contrary! He was always first to arrive and last to leave. He would never have read a newspaper or hid a novel behind his blotter nor gone to the WC for a smoke. Nor did he ever make up stories about some family crisis to wangle a day off. Never a dead grandmother nor a sick wife . . . Actually he was too conscientious . . .'

'What do you mean?'

'He was *obsessed with having a clear conscience*. Perhaps he got it from his early years, because I am aware that he was raised in a municipal orphanage. He constantly felt that he was being watched, that people weren't pleased with him and even suspected him. It made him touchy, and I could never quite bring myself to reprimand him because he was so sensitive . . . He was not liked by his colleagues. He lived in his little corner, did his work but never got on with the rest of the staff.'

'Tell me, Monsieur Drouin, had you already noticed that there was money missing from his drawer?'

The man of business looks startled.

'Money? . . . From his drawer? . . . No, that is quite impossible, inspector. Our practice rules out any possibility that anyone, not even our most senior employees, not even my chief clerk himself . . . We are not a shop with a till into which anyone can dip a hand when no one's looking. I can almost guarantee that actual money, cash, never passes through these offices. We sell buildings, chateaux, houses, building land. All our transactions run to hundreds of thousands of francs and, more often than not, millions. It is hardly necessary for me to add that payments of this kind are always made by cheque and almost invariably in the presence of a notary. As for buildings which we manage, the arrangements are more or less the same, and when due date settlements are not paid by cheque, then it is the job of our own cashier to . . .'

'So you're saying that it would have been quite impossible for your clerk to steal a thousand francs?'

'*Strictly impossible* . . . Furthermore, as I have told you, Mascouvin's character . . . No, inspector! . . . You are barking up the wrong tree . . . I'm sorry, but . . .'

He gets to his feet and intimates that he has important clients waiting.

'Just one other small question, which I think does not

infringe client confidentiality. Is Monsieur Blaise a big client here?'

Drouin hesitates. But to get rid of this policeman he is prepared to answer.

'A big client, no. His bank references are certainly excellent. Details of that sort you would be given by any financial agency. But a big client in our terms, no. More a nuisance, actually, without wishing to say anything to his detriment. It's the sort of thing that often happens . . . especially with investors who have nothing much to do with their time. For them it's a hobby . . . He turns up. He asks about current operations, he goes and views land and houses for sale, argues about prices as if he were buying. Most of the time, he does not make up his mind . . . As a matter of fact . . .'

He takes out a manila file with the name of Monsieur Blaise and a number on it.

'Over a period of five years, he has, through us, acquired three properties: a modest house, a small farm in Brittany and an apartment block in Nice. Total cost, six hundred thousand francs . . . And that, inspector, is all I am able to tell you . . . You must forgive me, but my time, like yours, is valuable . . .'

He does not hold out his hand and closes the door behind Maigret with evident relief.

Why on earth did Mascouvin, who was not being questioned about any such thing, put his hand up to stealing a thousand francs from his employer?

It is a worried Maigret who walks into his office. The clerk informs him that the examining magistrate has been waiting for him for more than an hour. Someone else who must be getting impatient, thinking that the case is dragging on, talking about the press and the adverse coverage, and wanting action.

Pipe in mouth, Maigret heads straight for the corridor where the offices of the examining magistrates are located. It is crowded with remand prisoners with police escorts, and witnesses who keep looking at their watches, all waiting in a hothouse atmosphere.

'Come in, detective chief inspector. Have a seat. I have read the report you submitted yesterday evening very carefully. We discussed it this morning with the deputy public prosecutor. He shares my view completely. Either this Octave Le Cloaguen of yours . . .'

Why *of yours*?

'Either this Octave Le Cloaguen of yours is really mad or else, if he is not guilty, which I am beginning to doubt, he knows a lot more than he is saying. Which is why I have this morning issued an order notifying him that at three o'clock this afternoon he is to be examined by two psychiatrists assisted by Dr Paul . . . What is your view?'

He is sure of himself. It is almost as if he is challenging the inspector, as if he is saying: 'Of course, it is well known that you have your methods. But they are slow, my dear Maigret! They are antiquated. An examining magistrate is not necessarily a fool, and, without leaving his desk, he can get to the bottom of cases which leave the police floundering . . .'

Maigret smokes his pipe in silence. It is impossible to read his thoughts.

'At the same time, I sent a rogatory commission to

Saint-Raphaël, asking them to gather information about the kind of life the Le Cloaguens led there . . .'

Maigret's failure to respond is making him nervous. Is the inspector about to take umbrage at this interference and let him get on with it all by himself?

'Sorry about this. I'm sure you'll agree that with cases like these, which drag on, stir up public opinion and . . .'

'You have acted very helpfully, sir. But I wonder . . .'

'What?'

'Nothing . . . I'm probably wrong . . .'

The truth is that he is worried. In his mind's eye he can see the old man in his office the evening before, the clenched hands, tears rolling down his cheeks and with that helpless look which seems to be pleading for a little warmth and kindness from a fellow human being.

How curious: the examining magistrate hadn't been so wrong from the start after all when he'd said 'this Octave Le Cloaguen *of yours*' . . .

'What time did he receive the summons to appear?'

'Let's see . . . It's eleven now . . . The special messenger must have rung the bell in Boulevard des Batignolles at about ten thirty . . .'

'Where will the psychiatric examination take place?'

'In the Le Cloaguens' apartment in the first instance. If the medics think it necessary, they'll take the old man to one of their clinics. Will you be there?'

'It's possible.'

'In that case, detective chief inspector, I shall see you later . . .'

It's true, Maigret is more than a little put out that anyone should have thought fit to take such a step without consulting him. Still, it is the case that he was late getting to Quai des Orfèvres and that he had been sent for . . .

But that is not all that is making him more weary, more disgruntled. It seems to him . . . How could it be put? . . . *His* Le Cloaguen . . . Yes, that's it! . . . It seems to him that he is the only one who can lay bare the strange old man's soul . . . From the start, from his visit to Rue Coulaincourt, he has been unsettled by the man, and he thinks about him all the time, whatever he is doing. He was thinking about him earlier when he discovered that Picpus was a vulgar, winking travesty, and still thinking about him in Monsieur Drouin's office whereas all his thoughts seemed to be about Mascouvin and Monsieur Blaise.

'Come in here, Lucas . . .'

Lucas is almost certainly aware of the measures which have been taken, for he does not look his chief directly in the eye.

'Who's on duty in Boulevard des Batignolles this morning? . . .'

'Janvier . . .'

As he stands before the wide-open window, a couplet learned by heart at school comes back to him unexpectedly:

> Though storm at sea may rage no more
> The sailor's widow weeps by the shore.

Isn't that also true in some degree of himself? The Seine flows on, wrapped in a veritable aura of absolute glory. The spectacle of pedestrians scuttling like ants is enough to make it seem as if the whole of Paris has surrendered to the sheer joy of being alive. Elsewhere anglers are fishing, the swimming pools are crowded with bathers, a symphony of car horns fills streets and boulevards and rises with the fine, golden dust into a sky of perfect blue.

Though storm at sea . . .

What a strange job he does! Two strikes with a knife in the back of a woman he has never met . . . An old man who sweats with fear . . . A clerk who jumps off the Pont-Neuf into the Seine . . . A calendar of stunning vulgarity in a café in Place de la République . . .

'What do we do now, sir?'

'What about Monsieur Blaise?'

'Around now he'll be heading to the Stock Exchange, just as he does every day . . . Ruel is tailing him . . .'

The search for the green convertible and the dark man with the gold teeth has drawn a blank. Emma, the girl from the dairy, spends every day with an eye on the street, where she still hopes to see her handsome motorist drive up, and has failed to recognize him in any of the photographs she has been shown.

'Will you get me the travel agent's near the Madeleine . . .'

He is still worried. He picks up the phone.

'Hello? . . . Mademoiselle Berthe? . . . It's Maigret . . . Yes . . . No, no . . . On the contrary . . . He's getting along well, give him a few days and he'll be over it . . . What time do you finish work? . . . Twelve? . . . Would you find it too dull to have lunch with me in some small restaurant near you? . . . Didn't catch . . . Good . . . I'll see you later . . .'

He takes a taxi and gets out at the hour when, as on most days of the week, workers from the offices around the Madeleine and the Boulevards are flooding out into the streets. He soon spots the little red hat and the fresh face with dimples, which now has a careworn look.

'You can take it from me, nothing terrible is happening . . . It was just that I wanted to talk to you . . .'

Passers-by turn to look at the two of them and tell each other that there's one middle-aged man who has the luck of the devil . . .

'Do you like hors-d'oeuvres?'

'Very much . . .'

He chooses a small restaurant frequented by regulars, which has a wide selection of tasty hors-d'oeuvres. They find a table near the window. It could be a cosy tête-à-tête and all the more so because Maigret orders a bottle of Alsace wine, the long neck of which rises out of an ice-bucket.

'Tell me, Mademoiselle Berthe, after your parents died and you continued your studies with financial help from Mascouvin . . . Would you like a few mushrooms? . . . As I was saying . . . I assume he paid for you to board some-where?'

'With nuns, at Montmorency.'

'That must have been expensive, I imagine?'

'I felt very bad about it. I knew he didn't earn much. But he believed he owed so much to our family. I'm sure there were times when he skipped meals so that he could pay for my keep . . .'

'You stayed there until what age?'

'Eighteen . . . As I told you, I wanted to live with him, it would have been cheaper, but he wouldn't hear of it. It was then that he began renting a small apartment for me in Les Ternes.'

'Furnished, I assume?'

'No. He wasn't keen on furnished apartments. He reckoned they don't do anything for a girl's reputation and said they are always fairly sad places and not very clean.'

'That was around five years ago,' murmured Maigret.

'That's correct. You've worked it out. I'm twenty-three now . . .'

'Tell me, would you mind very much after lunch showing an old gent like me round the apartment?'

'I'd love to . . . But I don't see . . . What shall I tell the concierge?'

'Tell her I'm a friend of Mascouvin . . . She does know, I suppose, that he is really more or less your half-brother? . . . Oh please, do eat up. I'm spoiling your appetite with all my absurd questions . . .'

Other men, the same age as him, are also having lunch in the restaurant with women as young and almost as attractive.

'But you must . . . I insist you choose a dessert . . .'

Someone waves a greeting, someone he doesn't know or rather doesn't recognize straight away, and he waves back. It is a few minutes later when he remembers the man, a more than shady banker he has sent to the Santé prison on two separate occasions.

Taxi . . . The girl looks at her watch . . .

'We'll have to be quick. I have to be back in the office at two.'

A quiet street after all the bustle of Place des Ternes.

'This is it. There's a lift.'

On the fifth floor, three rooms, minute certainly, but bright and cheerful and entirely consistent with Mademoiselle Berthe's youth.

'As you see, it's very simple. I didn't want him to go to the expense. But he said it was a bargain and that he'd persuaded the landlord to let him pay in monthly instalments . . .'

Maigret was expecting to find department store furniture but it proves to be otherwise. It is not great luxury, but every piece is of good quality . . . Twenty thousand? . . . Twenty-five? . . .

'Would you like to see the kitchen? I cook for myself in the evening. The sink has hot water. And instead of dustbins . . .'

Proudly she slides open a panel to reveal a kind of large waste disposal duct.

'It's quarter to two . . . If the bus doesn't come straight away . . .'

'I'll take you back in a taxi.'

'You mustn't drop me at the door . . . My work colleagues might think . . .'

Mascouvin . . . Le Cloaguen . . . Mascouvin . . . Le Cloaguen . . . Those are the two names which invariably thrust themselves to the forefront of Maigret's mind. Even when he tries to focus on the man with the brace of pike. The figure of Monsieur Blaise is always pushed to the back, effaced, perhaps because the inspector has not detected the same human vulnerability in him?

'Thanks for the lovely lunch, inspector . . . You are sure, aren't you, that Joseph? . . .'

At tables outside cafés, people are busy digesting over-ample lunches. Others, in packed buses, are heading for the race-courses.

Preferring to walk, because he is in no hurry, Maigret strolls up Boulevard Malesherbes, along Avenue de Villiers and reaches Boulevard des Batignolles at about two thirty. He looks around briefly for Janvier.

The latter calls to him from a small lorry-drivers' café-restaurant, where he is sitting at a table with the remains of lunch and a glass of calvados in front of him.

'Fancy a calva, sir? It's not bad. Nothing much to report this morning. The old man went out for his walk as usual at about eight thirty and, after finding a local uniformed officer to keep an eye on the house, I followed. We covered a lot of ground at a leisurely amble, as far as the Bois de Boulogne and back via the Porte Maillot . . . He returned home with-out speaking to anybody at a few minutes before noon.'

'What does the man in uniform say?'

'I questioned him before I took over from him. The ladies haven't gone out. Meat and vegetables were delivered. They must have phoned their orders to their usual sup-pliers. Around ten, a messenger on a bike from the Palais de Justice . . .'

'I know . . .'

'In that case you know everything. It was quite late when

I came in here because there's a building site round the corner, and the men working on it come here to eat. There wasn't a table free. I went out and phoned in from Place Clichy . . . What do you make of this calvados? Quite decent, isn't it? I always think that it's lorry-drivers' cafés where you . . .'

A car pulls up outside the house opposite. Maigret stands up.

'I'll let you pay. I'll see you later . . .'

'You want me to stay here?'

'Yes.'

A second car follows closely behind the first. In it are two middle-aged men and a strapping fellow who must be a nurse. He carries a voluminous medical case. From the first vehicle steps the examining magistrate accompanied by Dr Paul, the police pathologist.

'Ah, Maigret! Hello! . . . I didn't know I'd find you here . . . So . . . Is he mad? Is he not mad? You must have an opinion . . . How are you, Professor? . . . Hello, Delavigne . . . What happened about the man who'd lost his memory? Trying it on, was he?'

They exchange greetings on the pavement. Introductions are made. The mood is good-humoured, and no one would suspect these sober, elderly men are there to rule whether a fellow human being should remain at liberty or not.

'Shall we go up? You lead the way, detective chief inspector, you've been here before . . .'

The stained-glass windows lining the staircase sprinkle their faces with colour. There are splashes of blood red and other hues that gleam like bright gold coins. Maigret rings the bell. A sound of footsteps inside the apartment. Eventually the door opens.

'After you, gentlemen,' says the inspector, standing to one side.

Madame Le Cloaguen repeats:

'Do come in . . .'

What is wrong? She seems uneasy. She shows them into the drawing room. Then she turns to Maigret, the only one of the visitors she knows.

'Where is he?'

'Who do you mean? These gentlemen, as you know, have come to examine your husband's mental state. You have received a notification to that effect, which was sent to you by the examining magistrate, who is here . . .'

'Is that what it was?'

'Come now, madame. This morning, at about ten o'clock, while Monsieur Le Cloaguen was out on his walk, a messenger on a bicycle handed you an official letter . . .'

'Yes . . . but it was addressed to my husband.'

'You didn't open it? . . . Don't you know what it said?'

'I am not in the habit of reading letters which are not addressed to me. I put the envelope down – it was yellow as I remember – here . . . See for yourself . . .'

She opens the door, points to a low antique table in the hallway, and there indeed, under it, they see the yellow envelope with the prosecutor's office's name printed on it. It is empty.

'What happened?'

'I have no idea. My husband came back from his walk, as usual, for lunch . . .'

'Did he read the letter?'

'I imagine he did since neither I nor my daughter opened it. The three of us had lunch together. I don't even know if the dining table has been cleared . . . No . . . Our maid is on holiday . . .'

She opens another door to the dining room. Three places can be seen still laid, a bowl of fruit and remnants of a cheese board.

'You can see for yourselves. Afterwards, I thought Octave went for a nap in his room. He keeps very much to himself . . . very much . . .'

She is patently not afraid of irony, given that it is her custom to shut the old man up by himself like some naughty schoolboy!

'Is he not in his room?'

'I just looked . . . No . . . Moreover, his overcoat is not hanging on the hallstand. He must have gone out . . .'

'What time did you last see him?'

'We finished lunch at a quarter to one. We eat early. But won't you tell me what these gentlemen . . .'

Maigret directs a bitter smile at the examining magistrate. Madame Le Cloaguen remains perfectly composed.

'You must know where he is better than I do, because a watch is kept on our house from dawn to dusk and from dusk to dawn!'

The inspector crosses to the window and sees Janvier on the pavement opposite, picking his teeth as he stares up at the house.

The patience of the two psychiatric specialists begins to wear thin, and, since there is no patient for them to examine, they ask if they might leave and get back to their work.

The magistrate is baffled. He asks:

'Are you quite sure, madame, that he is not in the apartment?'

As loftily as her diminutive stature permits she replies:

'If you're in a muddle, there's nothing preventing you from searching the premises . . .'

An hour later, the fact has to be faced: *Octave Le Cloaguen, his greenish overcoat and his hat have disappeared.*

7. The Inspector Says Nothing

No, sir, you, the examining magistrate, must not think for one moment that Maigret is trying to get even. Surly he isn't, furious he is not: Maigret is worried. Maigret has a weight on his shoulders and yet he also feels that he is beginning to understand. That is why he says nothing!

As examining magistrate, you keep talking, talking, to hide your discomfiture, to ensure that eventually someone will tell you that you're in the right or at the very least that you weren't exactly wrong.

Maigret does not resent the over-confidence you showed this morning nor the faintly ironic self-satisfaction with which you told him of the steps you had taken.

'You don't run a police force by employing choirboys . . .'

Nor do you hand over the investigation of a crime to a little girl. And, in terms of character, a little girl is what you are next to Maigret. Books have taught you a great many things about human nature. You could reel them off by heart, but none of that counts, and what proves it is that only a short while ago you turned bright red and even now you are still shaking.

'Look here, Maigret, it's simply impossible that the man living in that room isn't mad . . . Admit it . . .'

Why? Why mad? In the course of his thirty years in the job, Maigret has seen all kinds of everything. He has sniffed the air and smelled the odour of human passions, vices, crimes and manias, the entire ferment of massed humanity.

'A man in possession of his faculties who owns a comfortable, I'd go so far as to say luxurious, apartment and has had a fulfilling career, who then allows himself to be . . .'

Maigret says nothing.

Ever since the mental specialists left, after the last hand had been shaken, the examining magistrate has been busying around, while Madame Le Cloaguen and her daughter have remained in the drawing room, putting themselves entirely at his disposal.

It was the judge who sent for Inspector Janvier, who was on duty in Boulevard des Batignolles. He questioned Janvier himself.

'Tell me, officer, are you sure you never took your eyes off the front door of this building?'

'All except for about a quarter of an hour. A little after twelve thirty. I had to go and phone the Police Judiciaire with my report . . .'

'Well, my friend, that was a serious mistake. You should have found some other way of reporting in. I have no idea how, that's for you to work out, but keeping watch means watching all the time and . . .'

Maigret does not even raise a smile. All this is so irrelevant!

'I assume you've been sufficiently curious to ask the concierge if there's another way out of the building?'

'There isn't one, sir.'

'Tell me, Maigret, I've just had an idea. Not that I have

any doubt that Le Cloaguen, sensing that we were on to him, slipped away while your officer was away phoning. But in so serious a case as this, we cannot afford to overlook the smallest lead. Your inspector might consider talking to all the tenants in the building and asking if they would allow him, not to search their premises, but to have a quick look round . . . Keep it friendly, mind . . .'

Maigret remains silent. Having his hands in his pockets, he has let his pipe go out, something which happens rarely, and while the magistrate continues to fuss, he stares at the greyish floor.

At this point Janvier returns from doing the rounds through the building unsurprisingly empty-handed. The magistrate becomes increasingly flustered.

'It is vital we get our hands on this man! . . . Do you realize, Maigret, that a madman, *a madman who has already killed once*, is on the loose in the streets of Paris!'

He summons Madame Le Cloaguen.

'Tell me, madame, does your husband have any money with him?'

'No.'

'Are you sure?'

'Certain.'

'Hear that, Maigret? He hasn't any money on him! Well, he'll have to eat. By this evening, he'll be hungry. He'll have to sleep somewhere! Where will he get the money for that from? Do you follow my drift? Madame, could you let me have a photo of your husband?'

Maigret says nothing, and there is something ominous in his silence. The examining magistrate thinks only in terms of dramatic methods such as publishing the photo in all the newspapers with circulations in the thousands, which can then be given to all uniformed police in towns and country as well as to passport officers at frontier control points . . .

'I know of no photograph of my husband . . .'

'But surely . . . We wouldn't necessarily need a large portrait or even a recent likeness . . . You must have . . . That's it! His passport, for example . . .'

'My husband has not left France for thirty years. His passport has not been renewed. It has probably been lost. If you cannot find it in his room, then it no longer exists.'

The magistrate glances at Maigret and sees a flicker of something in the inspector's eyes, but he does not understand its significance, and if he did he would immediately put a stop to all this pointless activity.

'Maigret, I want you to phone through a description of Octave Le Cloaguen to Records and tell them to . . .'

Of course he will do it! Maigret will do whatever he's asked. Without giving it a second thought. But he has a real sense of dramas which are being acted out in places which are not the streets of Paris or frontier control points.

On his way to the phone, which is fixed to a wall in the hallway, he feels the eyes of Madame Le Cloaguen on him and as he passes a door he catches a glimpse of the figure of Gisèle Le Cloaguen and he remembers . . .

He remembers the taxi and the drop of sweat which fell on to the old man's hand from the perspiration beading his forehead . . .

Exactly when had that happened? *It happened when, and only when, the taxi was nearing the house in Boulevard des Batignolles!*

While the old man was near the body in Rue Coulaincourt, in the flat where the splashes of blood were still fresh, he hadn't been afraid. He'd looked crushed but not afraid.

And last evening, in Maigret's office on Quai des Orfèvres, he seemed to welcome with some relief the prospect of being arrested!

'Hello? . . . Records? . . . Is that you, Maniu . . . Will you take down this description and put it out through all the usual channels? . . . The man must be approached with caution and apprehended on sight . . . Yes, the examining magistrate insists he should be described as extremely dangerous.'

At the other end of the line, Maniu relishes to the full the irony of those words, for he knows exactly what Maigret thinks of examining magistrates who interfere in criminal investigations.

'Did you let him get away?'

'*Seems we did . . .*'

The wife is standing behind him. He turns and glares so coldly that she is unable to repress a shiver of fear.

Outside, the magistrate is emphatic:

'I am literally terrified by the thought that this man is out there somewhere, probably armed, and determined to save his skin at any price. You must admit, Maigret, that it is most unfortunate that your officer should have sloped off to phone in! We had him! We had the murderer! The very fact that he escaped proves that he's guilty. But now . . . Are you going back to Quai des Orfèvres? . . .'

'I'm not sure . . .'

'What are you thinking of doing?'

'I don't know yet . . .'

'This has been one in the eye for you, hasn't it . . .'

What would be the point of undeceiving him? Maigret holds his tongue! He also says nothing when a crestfallen Janvier joins him on the pavement, or more accurately, later, when they are sitting in front of a beer apiece on the terrace of the little café-restaurant opposite. Then he murmurs:

'Mustn't take it to heart, Janvier . . .'

'All the same, sir, when there's going to be fireworks . . .'

'If there was going to be a row, it's already happened . . .'

'Got an idea?'

Silence from Maigret. He fills his pipe, lights it and watches the match burn out.

'I'm wondering if I've got time . . .' he sighs eventually, stretching his legs out like a man exhausted.

'Time for what?'

'To go down to Saint-Raphaël.'

'Can't you send someone?'

But that is exactly what is just not possible. Of course, a junior officer can be entrusted with a specific task. But how can he be told that he . . . How can he be ordered to go there and search around like a dog grubbing through refuse and do whatever it takes to sniff out the bone, or rather the secret which . . .

Maigret is warming to this theme. A curtain twitches in a window in the house opposite. Two eyes stare at the inspector across the boulevard, the eyes of a woman, and they too are full of fear.

What thought has just entered his mind out of the blue? He was staring at the face at the window. The face has now vanished, and suddenly Maigret relaxes.

'Right, I want you to go across the road . . . Park yourself on the stairs, just outside the door, and don't move from there for any reason. It doesn't matter if you're seen . . . Got that?'

'What if one of the women comes out?'

'Let her . . . Don't stir from there!'

After ensuring his order has been carried out, he goes inside the café.

'Do you have a phone?'

The phone is in the bar itself, which explains why, when the place was full of customers, Inspector Janvier preferred to use a more private phone booth, in a café on Place Clichy.

'Lucas? . . . Say again . . . Absolutely not! It doesn't matter, my friend . . . As long as it keeps the public prosecutor's people happy . . . Jump into a car . . . Yes . . . Boulevard des Batignolles . . . The café-restaurant across the road . . . I'll wait for you there . . .'

The owner of the café gives him a curious look, wondering what has brought the police to his neck of the woods, because he has no doubt who these men are.

'Hello, operator, get me Saint-Raphaël . . . I don't know

the number . . . The name is Larignan, a lawyer . . . That's all I know . . . This is a police priority . . .'

It's definitely a day for beer. There are already four markers on the table out on the terrace by the time there's a reply from Saint-Raphaël.

'Hello? . . . I'm the maid . . . No, sir . . . Yes, sir . . . No, sir . . . Monsieur Larignan, is out . . . What? . . . Yes, sir, he's probably gone down to the pier, to paint . . . Who wishes to speak to him? . . . The police? . . . Very good, sir . . . I'll go at once . . .'

In his mind's eye he sees her leaving the gleaming white, well-to-do villa, braving the sun of the Côte d'Azur, which picks out the chalky flecks of sails in the bay, in search of the lawyer who has erected his easel on the jetty and is surrounded by curious onlookers.

'What will you drink, Lucas? . . . Landlord, could we have a couple of beers here?'

Lucas sees immediately that this is not the moment for questions. An hour goes by while poor Janvier twiddles his thumbs on the step of a staircase and leaps to his feet each time a tenant passes.

The phone rings.

'Monsieur Larignan? . . . What? . . . No, Monsieur Larignan, your wife hasn't been involved in an accident . . . I don't even know where your wife is! . . . In Vichy, taking the waters? . . . It's very good for the health . . . But tell me . . . When exactly did Monsieur Le Cloaguen . . . Yes, your client, Monsieur Le Cloaguen, when precisely, I repeat, did he stop signing a receipt for the money which you paid to him? . . . Yes, yes, as you can see I know all about it . . .

No need to worry . . . Why am I phoning you from a restaurant since I'm from the police? . . . Because I don't have time to go back to Quai des Orfèvres . . . You are very suspicious, Monsieur Larignan . . . Yes, I'm listening . . . About ten years ago? . . . Yes . . . After his accident? . . . And am I correct in thinking that it was then that the family left Saint-Raphaël? . . .'

He dabs at his forehead. The man on the other end of the phone in the Midi plays his cards close to his chest. The words have to be dug out of him one by one, not an easy thing to do on the phone.

'How was this income of 200,000 francs paid? . . . I see . . . You yourself came to Paris each year? . . . In cash? . . . Don't cut us off, operator . . . Listen, do that if you like but don't cut us off, for the love of God just don't cut us off! . . . Are you still there, Monsieur Larignan? . . . Did you give the money to Monsieur Le Cloaguen himself? . . . What was that? . . . I understand . . . It was laid down in the terms of the deed of gift? . . . Obviously . . . Yes . . . Yes . . .'

The lawyer in Saint-Raphaël is even more suspicious than seems possible! As he says, or rather bellows, into the phone, because he is one of those men who believe that they can be heard more clearly if they shout into the receiver, it was his duty to make sure that his client was still alive on the payment date.

'And you saw him each time? . . . Yes, I understand . . . Was he in bed? . . . No? . . . Ill, but not in bed? . . . That's it exactly . . . Mainly he had lost weight . . . Yes . . . Speak freely, you can be frank . . . Yes . . . Obviously it's odd . . .

Odd . . . A crank, yes . . . At his age . . . Of course . . . One more thing . . . The house they lived in . . . Sold? . . . It's not occupied at present? . . . An American woman who comes to France every two or three years? . . . And you have the keys? . . . I would be most grateful if you would let the person I shall send to you have them . . . No need to worry . . . You'd be covered by an order from the public prosecutor's department, which will be wired through . . . I am most grateful, Monsieur Larignan . . . I'd rather not . . . Better stay at home, I might need to phone you again . . .

'Bring me a beer! . . .'

His expression is already more open that it was. He even manages a faint smile as he sits down and says to Lucas, who is waiting patiently:

'Now there's a funny thing . . . Guess what Le Cloaguen was doing one day when Monsieur Larignan brought him his 200,000 francs? . . . He was studying French grammar! . . . In the drawing room, just he and his wife, who seemed to be teaching him and looked very put out.'

'I don't see what . . .'

'Wait! . . . It wouldn't surprise me that before this evening . . . But now I must phone our excellent examining magistrate, who will tell me to go to blazes . . .'

The small lorry-drivers' café-restaurant has turned into a kind of general headquarters. It is as if Maigret is reluctant to lose eye contact with the tall, grey building with the carriage entrance where a curtain twitches from time to time.

'Hello? . . . I'm sorry to bother you, sir . . . No, nothing significant as yet . . . I'd like you to wire a telegraphic order to Saint-Raphaël . . . Authorization to receive from a lawyer, Monsieur Larignan, the keys of a certain property . . . And preferably a recommendation to send along a mason and a couple of workmen . . . Dangerous? . . . Yes . . . I know . . . Of course, when she gets back, the owner will kick up a fuss, as you say . . . But I think it's necessary . . . Yes . . . Cellars, everything . . . The grounds, if there are grounds . . . The grotto, if there is one . . . The well . . . Everything, absolutely everything! . . . I'd like the response phoned through to me here . . . Thank you, sir . . .'

Is this his fifth or sixth beer? Imperceptibly, Maigret is becoming a different man. It is as if he is getting ready for action, that all his faculties have become sharper, that he is proceeding straight ahead with quiet, disciplined power.

'What am I to do now, sir?' asks Lucas.

'Go and buy a paper . . .'

The newspaper has already published the description of Octave Le Cloaguen.

A dangerous lunatic who was probably responsible for the murder of the clairvoyant in Rue Coulaincourt, is at large in the capital . . .

Maigret shrugs his shoulders. As long as it amuses the examining magistrate, the papers and the public! . . .

'Do you think he's got away?'

'No . . .'

'But if that's so . . .'

'Yes, my friend . . . Maybe he has, maybe he hasn't . . .'

'What about the two women?'

'No idea . . . Come on . . . Landlord, what do I owe you? If there's a phone call for me from Saint-Raphaël or Quai des Orfèvres, come and get me at the double. I'll be in the house across the road . . .'

He has tried not to act so precipitately, to hold back, to wait for as long as it takes, but if Le Cloaguen is not dead . . .

To the concierge he says:

'Good morning, madame. It's me again. Tell me, I imagine each of your tenants has a cellar? Would you show us the way? A torch? You're very kind. Yes, bring a torch . . .'

They go down one behind the other. In a huge vaulted cellar all the tenants have their own space enclosed by an iron railing through which coal and old packing cases are visible.

'No . . . No need to bother the ladies . . . The lock's child's play, as you'll see . . .'

And so it is. He opens it in a matter of minutes. Empty sacks which had contained potatoes. A load of logs recently delivered. A little coal left over from last winter.

'Do you have a shovel, madame?'

'You'll get dirty . . .'

So what? Maigret digs into the pile of coal, just in case. Then, with the same patience, he inspects all the bunkers belonging to the other tenants.

'I'll be careful not to, madame . . . The Le Cloaguens don't have a maid, but I assume, judging by the size of their apartment, they have one or two maids' rooms?'

'Yes, on the seventh floor. They've got two . . .'

'May I ask you to come up with us?'

'Only if I can turn the gas down under my stew, otherwise it'll be burned when I come back down again . . .'

Janvier, looking glum, stands up to let them pass. The concierge turns round, overawed by the gravity of what is being enacted.

'They were going to put a lift in, but then they saw it wasn't possible seeing as how the stairwell isn't wide enough . . .'

Up here the layout changes. A long corridor with varnished walls. Numbered doors. Daylight enters only through a fanlight.

'These are their rooms: 13 and 14 . . . Last year, they tried to rent them out but they were asking too much for what they are . . . Wait a minute . . . My master-key should work in these locks . . .'

Lucas, who has followed them, begins to feel apprehensive. The first room, where a musty smell catches the throat, contains only a folding bedstead, two old wobbly chairs and a chest full of odd volumes.

'It's what you might call abandoned,' said the concierge.

A similar disappointment in the second room. What was the inspector hoping to find? There's nothing except the same kind of jumble which every family drags around with them, a terrestrial globe, a seamstress's dummy, more books, especially medical books, and piles of fly-blown anatomical plates, with brown foxing.

'Empty! As you see!'

'Empty . . .' says Maigret, repeating the word, like an echo.

And yet he cannot bring himself to abandon the narrow corridor which leads nowhere.

'One other thing, madame. Why is there a ladder over the stairwell?'

'They might as well take it away, for all the use it gets. As you see, above the last three rooms there is a sort of loft. Certain tenants are allowed use of it to store the large trunks that they don't know what to do with. To get to the loft, you need a ladder . . .'

Maigret nods to Lucas, who goes off meekly to get it.

'Shall I go up, sir?'

'No.'

Maigret will climb up himself, and Lucas is a little scared.

'Listen, sir, it would be better if you . . .'

He holds out his revolver, which the inspector takes with a shrug of the shoulders.

When he is on the second rung and the whole ladder starts shaking under his weight, he changes his mind and steps off it again.

'He can't be dead,' he mutters.

'Why not?'

'Because I defy two women to hoist an inert body up this ladder.'

He looks up, the way an adult calls to a child who is stuck up a tree.

'Le Cloaguen! . . .' he cries. 'Le Cloaguen! . . .'

Silence. The concierge, alarmed, puts one hand over her bosom and stands ready for anything.

'Listen, Lucas, I hate ladders and I would be glad if you shinned up this one. It's not solid enough for me . . .'

A few more moments of silence.

'Shall I go up?'

A faint scraping sound. Someone up there has moved, someone who has brushed against some resonant object, probably an empty trunk. Then a leg appears, a foot feeling for a rung, and finally a man wearing a greenish overcoat climbs down the ladder.

No one could possibly imagine Maigret's feeling of triumphant exultation at this moment. Or rather, there is one man, Lucas, who glances across at his chief and would swear he can see tears brimming in his eyes.

Maigret has worked all this out by himself, without any clues it might be said, or more accurately by using clues which everyone else has missed, and in particular by drawing on his amazing intuition, his frightening ability to put himself in the shoes of other people.

'You've been lucky, Le Cloaguen! . . .'

The old man shows no sign of fear now. He stands there, almost indifferent, like a man who has fought to the bitter end and has become resigned to his fate. His only reaction is a sigh which perhaps is actually more a sigh of relief.

'If we hadn't come, I really think you'd have starved to death . . .'

The man clearly misconstrues the meaning of the words for, after a moment's hesitation, he stammers:

'Have you arrested them?'

He is covered with dust. In the loft, there is not enough room for a man to stand up in.

'Have you arrested them?'

Asked after what Maigret has said, does not the question mean:

'If what you say is true, that I'd have starved to death,

it must be because my wife and daughter are not in the house, since they were supposed to bring me something to eat.'

This is how Lucas understands the words and he gives his chief a look full of admiration.

'No, I haven't arrested them yet.'

The old man doesn't understand.

'You shall see for yourself . . . Come along! . . .'

They make their way down the stairs. On the third floor, they see Janvier sitting on a stair just by the door. He leaps to his feet.

'Now do you understand, Le Cloaguen? . . . *They wouldn't have dared bring you anything to eat, would they?* That's why I was forced to act today. But I would really have preferred to hang fire!'

A sound like scampering mice comes from behind the door. Maigret rings the bell and turns to the concierge.

'You can go back to your lodge, madame. I am most grateful to you . . . As you see, everything has gone very smoothly . . .'

The door half opens. A pointed nose. A pointed face. The sharp eyes of Madame Le Cloaguen. A screech.

'You found him! . . . Where was he? . . .'

'Come in Lucas! Come on in, Janvier! You can come in too, my dear fellow . . .'

Le Cloaguen gives a start on hearing the friendly expression which Maigret has called him by for the first time. He gives every appearance of liking it, that it relaxes him.

'See, I won't even be asking you to recite the rule governing the use of the past participle . . .'

Now it is the woman's turn to jump. She turns to the inspector as if she has just been bitten by an animal.

'What do you mean by that?'

'Nothing more, madame, than what I say . . . Lucas, don't let her out of your sight! Janvier, go and fetch the daughter and watch her every move. No need to bother about the old boy . . . That's right, friend, you'll behave yourself from now on, won't you?'

The strangest thing of all is the look of gratitude that the old man gives him.

'Can I take my overcoat off?' he asks.

'Of course you can . . . *It doesn't matter any more . . .*'

Even so, Maigret is intrigued by the manoeuvre. It is as if he is expecting some extraordinary revelation. It proves less momentous than he thought. Once the thick coat has been removed, it becomes clear that one shoulder must be heavily padded because it now emerges that the old man has one shoulder higher than the other.

Meanwhile, Lucas and Janvier cannot understand the jubilation of their chief, who knocks out his pipe on the carpet and refills another – the cold pipe he always keeps with him in reserve.

All six of them are in the drawing room with the dark furniture and green plush curtains, where the noise of Paris percolates through to them. They remain perfectly still, like the wax figures in the Musée Grévin, all save for the jerky movements of Madame Le Cloaguen's ringed hands.

The sound of heavy but hurried footsteps on the stairs. A man pauses uncertainly outside the door. Calmly, Maigret opens it.

'Phone, sir . . . Saint-Raphaël . . .'

The owner of the small café-restaurant is disconcerted by the frozen figures which peer at him in bewilderment. Maigret follows him back to the door.

'Listen here . . .'

He takes his time. He looks straight into the eyes of Madame Le Cloaguen.

'The first one of you who moves . . .'

And he gleefully taps his revolver pocket.

'I won't be long! . . .'

8. Madame Le Cloaguen's Revenge

From the public's point of view, it was far from being one of Maigret's most high-profile investigations, for the papers, having first stirred the pot vigorously, suddenly lost interest in the Rue Coulaincourt clairvoyant. At Quai des Orfèvres, on the other hand, every detail of the case and even certain comments, true or false, remain etched in people's memories and have become part of the lore of the place.

And so too did the storm which, around five that afternoon, burst over Paris, after a month of drought and heat.

'Never saw a storm like it in the whole of my life!' Sergeant Lucas again declares. 'Just imagine, there we were, in the drawing room with the green curtains, Janvier and me on the one side and the two women and the old man on the other . . .'

It is perhaps twenty minutes since Maigret went out hard on the heels of the owner of the café-restaurant on the other side of the road, and already Madame Le Cloaguen, becoming impatient, stands up and takes up a position by the window, one hand on the curtain in, surely, the same spot as when she watched the inspectors who had been put there to watch the house.

A gust of wind sweeps along Boulevard des Batignolles, raises swirls of dust as high as the windows on the third floor and tugs at café awnings. Suddenly the deluge breaks in a hissing roar; a moving tide flows over pavements while pedestrians can be seen scurrying this way and that and taxi-boats plough through the stream, spraying moustaches of water.

Madame Le Cloaguen's face, pressed hard against the window, is the only one to emerge distinctly from the semi-darkness that fills the room. Lucas is thinking of all the men unfortunate to marry such women, when she whirls round on him in a fury and, pointing to the boulevard, snaps:

'Where's he going?'

For Maigret has just come out of the small drivers' café-restaurant. Turning up the collar of his jacket, he is heading off quickly towards Place Clichy, clearly in search of a taxi.

At this point, the wife comes out with one of the remarks which will become classics at the Police Judiciaire:

'*I hope he hasn't forgotten us!*'

It's the first incident of note – a somewhat comic incident – in that memorable wait. Lucas, determined to be like Maigret in every respect, tranquilly fills his pipe, becomes aware that the old man is watching him, remembers that he chews tobacco and hands him his pouch . . .

'I must go to the smallest room . . .' breathes the old man with pale eyes. 'If you want to come with me . . .'

Of course he will! Lucas escorts him and even prevents him shutting the door.

'Would you like to come to my room for a moment?'

There, at the back of a cupboard, he extracts an old pipe with a broken stem from a worn-down shoe.

'Don't you see? . . . *They can't say anything now!* . . . Pass me back your pouch, will you?'

He is determined that it should happen in the drawing room, in full view of the two women. Taking his time, he fills his pipe, strikes a match on the box which the sergeant hands him.

Madame Le Cloaguen has reached the end of her patience.

'I really don't see why we are being kept waiting . . .'

Her frustrations, however, are only just beginning. The minutes tick by, and the room is slowly filled with a smell of old pipe. A shutter bangs against the front wall of the house, the rain hisses, pedestrians are still running through the streets or seeking shelter under carriage entrances, and then, just an hour later, a taxi pulls up outside, someone gets out, the feet of two people are heard on the stairs, and the electric bell rings. Janvier gets up and opens the door. It's the examining magistrate.

'Oh, it's you, sir! . . . Do come in . . . No, he isn't here . . . He went across the street to phone, then he ran off in the direction of Place Clichy . . .'

The examining magistrate, who is accompanied by a tall, gaunt officer of the court, sits down after acknowledging both women with an embarrassed nod, for he has not been put in the picture. Maigret hasn't told him anything but merely phoned through, asking him to go to Boulevard des Batignolles with his court officer.

The room, normally gloomy, has become positively crepuscular, and from time to time a brighter flash of lightning makes everyone jump. There they all are, cheek by jowl, stiff and unmoving as if they were sitting in a railway compartment, as silent as they would be in a doctor's waiting room. They watch each other. Lucas offers his tobacco pouch to the old man, who has smoked one pipe and now, with childish delight, sets about filling another.

Janvier looks at his watch, and his gesture will be the only movement, repeated by the magistrate or the court officer, to disturb the stillness.

Seven o'clock . . . Half past . . . Then suddenly the voice of Octave Le Cloaguen, still a little intimidated . . . It is to Lucas that he turns, as if the magistrate is too great a personage for him.

'There's some port in the sideboard . . . *But she's got the key . . .*'

Her eyes are full of hate. Without saying a word, Madame Le Cloaguen looks in her handbag for a key and places it on the small round table.

'A glass of port, madame?'

'No thank you . . .'

But the daughter, the more upset of the two, murmurs:

'I think I would, very much, just a drop . . .'

The situation has not changed at eight o'clock, when Lucas decides to switch on the light, for no one can see anything at all. Lucas is hungry. So is Janvier. The bell rings, and this time the sergeant opens it and is the first to hear Maigret's voice on the landing.

'Go in, madame . . .'

A small, elderly woman dressed very neatly, even smartly, in black, with a complexion that is surprisingly fresh for someone of her age, enters uncertainly. All these people sitting so motionless take her aback, and at first she sees only Madame Le Cloaguen. With both dark-gloved hands on her bag, which has a silver clasp, she takes two or three steps forwards and says in a voice which rankles with longstanding, unyielding animosities:

'Good evening, Antoinette . . .'

Maigret's clothes glint like a wet umbrella, and he leaves pools of water on the polished floor as he moves around. He does not explain. He merely gives a small nod to the magistrate and the court officer.

'If this gentleman, who is very kind, had not insisted on me coming, after everything that's happened . . .'

But then she half turns and at last catches sight of the old man. She opens her mouth to speak, to say hello, but nothing emerges from her mouth; she screws up her eyes, she opens her handbag with feverish haste and takes out a pair of spectacles.

She gives the impression of being nonplussed, that she feels she is the victim of a hoax. Her eyes seek out first Maigret, then Antoinette Le Cloaguen, and then again come to rest on the old man, who does not understand what is happening any more than she does.

'That's not Octave! . . . You know very well that he's not my brother! . . . My God! . . . And there's me, who always wondered . . .'

'Take a seat, madame . . .' says Maigret, who adds, turning to the examining magistrate: 'I have the honour to introduce you to Madame Biron, née Catherine Le Cloaguen, a widowed lady whose existence has been revealed to me by the police at Saint-Raphaël. Do sit down, madame, there's no need to worry about the priest, because we shan't detain you for long . . .

'I must tell you, sir, that Madame Biron, who was left almost penniless on the death of her husband – a strong, good man, who worked for Saint-Raphaël town council – Madame Biron, then, became housekeeper to an elderly priest who was virtually incapable of looking after himself . . . She cares for him with quite admirable dedication . . .

'Now, Madame Biron, would you like to tell us about your brother, Octave?'

The two women try to catch each other's eye, and the priest's housekeeper, taking her time, speaks in short sentences and the hushed tones of one who has spent a lot of time in churches:

'Our parents weren't well off. They were good people. It was only by scrimping and scraping, as the saying goes, that they managed to put my brother through medical school . . . He travelled the world. He was lucky enough to do a good turn for a very rich man who proved to be very grateful . . . At that point, he got married, and I must admit he was very generous to us . . .'

'Just a moment . . . Do you mean that he used to send you money regularly?'

'Not regularly. My late husband wouldn't have accepted that. But he used every opportunity to help us out . . . Like the time I had my bad attack of bronchitis fifteen years ago, he arranged for me to stay in his villa in Saint-Raphaël, but I soon got the idea that I wasn't wanted . . .'

Everyone present also gets the idea from the look she shoots at Madame Le Cloaguen.

'My brother's voice didn't count for very much in his own house. I think he missed the time when he used to sail on the Company's ships. He bought himself a little boat. His only interest was going out in it all by himself and fishing in the sea. That way, at least, he had some peace . . .'

'Did they seem comfortably off in the villa?'

'I think so. There were . . . let me think . . . two servants . . .'

'So you'd say, on the whole, a way of life as befits an income of 200,000 francs?'

'Perhaps, I suppose . . . Myself, I've never had 200,000 francs to spend . . .'

'Was your brother in good health?'

'Maybe a bit too florid in the face, but I don't think he was ill . . . What's happened to him?'

All eyes turn towards Madame Le Cloaguen, who purses her lips and maintains an angry silence.

'Would your brother's wife have stood to gain in any way by wanting to kill him?'

'You never can tell. But I don't think so, because the money would have gone on being paid only for as long as he was still alive . . .'

'Do you have anything to add, Madame Le Cloaguen?'

At that moment, Maigret feels the weight of the most hate-filled look that has ever been turned on him. It is so baneful that he cannot repress a smile.

'Very well! . . .' he declares and then, to the examining magistrate, he says: 'I'm now going to explain a few things, sir . . . Give me a glass of that, Lucas. Isn't there anything stronger in the house?'

The old man intervenes:

'There must be a half-bottle of cognac in her bed-room . . .'

Meaning, of course: in the bedroom of Antoinette Le Cloaguen.

'This is the story in a few words. At Saint-Raphaël, Le Cloaguen leads the easy life of a man who has 200,000 francs a year to spend. I phoned his bank. Ten years ago he had savings of no more than a few tens of thousands of francs. Then all of a sudden he dies unexpectedly. Maybe one day, his widow, Madame Le Cloaguen will be so good as to tell us what he died of . . . Did he get too much sun one day when out fishing and died of a stroke? . . .

'However that may be, his wife and daughter will no longer have any money coming in . . . There are people, sir, who cannot accept such a prospect . . .

'Now as it happens, there is a down-and-out who hangs around the marinas at Cannes, not very bright but not at all dangerous, who bears a striking resemblance to the retired ship's doctor . . .'

The counterfeit Le Cloaguen grins, in no way offended by the slighting judgement passed on his level of intelligence.

'A short while ago, gentlemen, the Saint-Raphaël police, following my directions, found the remains of the real Le Cloaguen walled up in one of the cellars in the villa. That's all I have. Or rather, there is just one more detail I should give you. When the offer of leading a comfortable and carefree life under another name was put to the tramp, and when the poor devil, fed up with hanging around the port and sleeping rough, agreed, there was an unexpected hitch: how would he sign the receipts for the money handed over by the solicitor each year without giving the game away? All attempts to teach him to copy the dead man's signature failed . . . I mean, he is hardly capable of writing his own name in a clumsy scrawl! . . .

'That is why they made him cut off the top joint of the index finger of his right hand, which would provide a reasonable excuse . . .

'Too many people know him on the Côte d'Azur. And so they decide to move to Paris . . .

'Le Cloaguen's sister would obviously spot the substitution. So a way is found so hurtful that, having her pride, she will never have anything to do with her brother and his family ever again . . .'

'This woman,' mutters Madame Biron, 'sent me a letter telling me I was a sponger. I wrote to my brother, but he never replied, and now I know why. At the time, I told myself that she had finally got him entirely under her thumb.'

'*Money!*' says Maigret. 'Don't you see? This entire case boils down to a sordid matter of money, the most squalid it has ever been my misfortune to encounter. Imagine, it involved making a body disappear. Then the somewhat lopsided shape of the tramp had to be modified, for unfortunately he had one shoulder higher than the other . . .

'The man can barely read. He is given lessons in French and arithmetic. People might well be shocked to meet a former ship's doctor who is so uncouth. He is made to appear not all there, half mad . . . The fact that he has lived in the Far East provides an excellent explanation . . .'

Maigret looks round him with a sudden feeling of disgust.

'The most depressing part of all this is that the money cannot be freely enjoyed. The second Le Cloaguen might die like the first, and there's no way a replacement could be found. So from now on, they count every penny. They have to set aside almost the entire annual sum of 200,000 francs. In this way, over a period of ten years, these women have saved almost a million and a half. That is correct, Madame Le Cloaguen, is it not? . . .'

'As for you, Picard . . .'

The old man seems shocked at being called by his real name.

'You sold your birthright for a mess of pottage. You have a roof over your head, it's true. You are fed, because it is vital that you be kept alive. But no smoking, because the original Le Cloaguen didn't smoke. No drinking, because he hated alcohol. No this or that . . . No everything! . . . You're like a dog on a leash, and the only fun you get is from wandering through the streets just like you used to, and then the minute you get back you get locked up. When the lawyer comes on his annual visitation, they put you to bed, they take good care of you, they make out that you're ill, and your room is kept as dark as possible.

'Even so, you managed to escape the vigilance of your jailers . . . For despite everything you managed to keep one thing secret.'

Picard becomes agitated and looks away. He is clearly

trying to hold back the tears which are welling up in his eyes.

'From a marriage in the dim and distant past you had a daughter. You discovered her here in Paris. Every week you went to see her. Your daughter had set herself up in Rue Coulaincourt as a clairvoyant . . .'

The same dusty light from the chandelier, the same great swathes of shadow, the faces blurred, like faces under the varnish of a painting in a museum. Maigret has stopped talking. The magistrate, visibly uneasy, crosses and uncrosses his legs and eventually says in an uncertain voice:

'Madame Le Cloaguen, did you kill Mademoiselle Jeanne?'

'It's not true!'

'Madame Le Cloaguen, did you follow your sham husband to Rue Coulaincourt and did you enter an apartment at number 67A?'

'It's not true!' she repeats.

'Do you admit that you walled up the body of your lawful husband in the cellar of your villa at Saint-Raphaël?'

'And if I did?'

'Do you admit that you have improperly received money which you were no longer entitled to receive?'

'I have no idea. It wasn't me who received the money. The solicitor gave it directly to this man, and that is no affair of mine . . . I know exactly what the risks are for me . . .'

'Dear Lord above!' stammers the priest's housekeeper, appalled by such an attitude.

And even those men here who have seen it all before

stare in amazement as Madame Le Cloaguen, bony and prickly, states calmly, like a woman who knows exactly what she is saying, has done her homework and taken every precaution:

'I am sure you are quite aware that I am not running much of a risk. A fine of between sixteen and fifty francs and anything from six days to two months in prison . . . Article 368 of the Penal Code . . .'.

She is very pleased with herself, so much so that she cannot prevent a faint quiver of pride from playing across her lips.

'I had no idea that this man had a daughter and that he went to see her . . . As for my husband, I fail to see the difference, from his point of view, between burial in a cemetery and . . .'.

'Stop it, you unfeeling woman!' cries Madame Biron, who can contain herself no longer. 'Don't you realize that you are a monster, that no one ever heard a woman, one of the good Lord's creatures, come out with such abominations! . . . When I think of poor Octave . . . I can't breathe, sir . . . Give me some air . . .'.

Indeed the blood has drained from her face, and there are beads of perspiration on her upper lip. Maigret opens the window. The green curtain swells, the breath of the wind blows on every face, and the din of the storm bursts savagely into the room, where no one moves.

'Over to you, Maigret,' the magistrate, intrigued, seems to say.

He has the impression that the inspector has lost his usual self-confidence. He smokes his pipe, slowly, stands in front of Madame Le Cloaguen, a bulky, formidable presence, with an expression that seems set in stone.

'You are absolutely right, madame. There's not much the courts can do to you. Still, this is the first time in the whole of my career that I have seen love of money taken to such extremes and trigger such ignoble actions . . . I would almost prefer it if you had killed Le Cloaguen in a fit of anger . . .'

There is a cry from behind him. It is Madame Biron, who cannot understand what is happening.

'I'm sorry, madame . . . But there are things which must be said . . . The examining magistrate has just spoken of the poor young woman who was murdered in Rue Coulaincourt in particularly disturbing circumstances. Of course, Madame Le Cloaguen has only to say the word to throw light on the whole business, and we would have our murderer in a matter of minutes . . . Am I wrong, madame?'

She glowers at him. She hesitates for a split second. Then her expression becomes harder still if that is possible and she pronounces one word:

'No! . . .'

'You have our attention . . .'

'I'll not say anything, do you hear . . .'

A sudden change comes over her: she erupts, she turns into a raging fury.

'Never, do you understand? . . . I will not say anything, because I hate you all, and you, Detective Chief Inspector Maigret, more than anybody! From the first day you set foot in this apartment and gave me that look I have hated, loathed you! . . . I won't say anything! You won't find anything! I shall serve my two months in prison, so be it, but you . . . you . . .'

'Who did you give the 200,000 francs to?'

'I won't say . . .'

She corrects herself, but it's too late.

'What 200,000 francs?'

'The 200,000 francs you arranged to be taken out of the bank last Saturday.'

She does not answer.

'Where did you go on Sunday between ten in the morning and four in the afternoon?'

She rakes him with a look of fierce irony. Maigret realizes that she has made no idle boast, that a woman like her is capable of keeping her mouth shut, that no amount of questioning will extract one word from her.

He turns to the examining magistrate.

'Would you be so good, sir, as to sign a warrant for the arrest of this woman and her daughter . . .'

'My daughter? . . . What has my daughter got to do with all this? . . . You're a magistrate, so you must know that you have no right to do this. I haven't killed anybody, even the inspector has conceded that . . . At the time when I buried my husband secretly, which is the only charge that can be made against me, my daughter was still a minor . . . She was a child and, I repeat, you have no right . . .'

Tragedy alternates with farce, minute by minute, second by second. Maigret is dealing with a woman determined to defend herself to the end with tooth and claw . . .

'I did not kill a woman who I never even knew existed!'

'So who did kill her?'

'I have no idea . . . I won't say anything . . . I hate you! . . . You are a monster! . . .'

By monster, she means Maigret, who pours himself a glass of cognac and wipes his forehead. And on him, never leaving him for an instant, is fixed the doubtful gaze of the examining magistrate, who only moments before thought the case was all wrapped up and now realizes that it has never been more delicately balanced.

'Lucas, take this old lady away.'

Maigret has used the world *old* deliberately, and it earns him another savage glare.

'Janvier, will you look after the daughter? . . . Look out! . . . Lucas . . . Janvier . . .'

For Madame Le Cloaguen has made a dash for the open window. But, contrary to what the inspector was fearing, she is not trying to do away with herself. She has reached such a pitch of frustration that she hopes to start a commotion, she intends to scream, call for help, without realizing that there's not a soul now on Boulevard des Batignolles, where the ground under the trees is furrowed with rivulets, like a relief map.

'Use handcuffs on her, Lucas . . . Janvier, close the window! . . .'

There is a laugh, a strained laugh, and it is just as dramatic. It's the old tramp, who can't stand the tension any longer, laughing till he cries to see the harpy who has terrorized him for so long grappling with the bantamweight sergeant, punching, scratching, kicking out at his legs.

How could he ever have imagined that one day . . .

'I want, I demand someone to ring at once for a lawyer

. . . You've no right . . . no one has the right . . .'

It was written that the evening's proceedings will not end without reaching the height of absurdity. The doorbell rings. The bell has been rung again . . . Maigret strides to the door and opens it . . .

'Oh, I'm sorry . . . Is my friend . . .'

A middle-aged lady in a flounced skirt, accompanied by a tall, shy young man. She stares in amazement at the curious assortment of guests who stand stock-still in the drawing room . . . Then she sees Madame Le Cloaguen and makes her way eagerly towards her, with a delighted smile on her face . . .

'Dear Antoinette! Just imagine, with this storm . . .'

She comes to a dead stop. The hands she was about to shake so fulsomely . . . How is it possible that handcuffs? . . .

'But . . . I don't . . .'

Then the penny drops. The men are police, and she, born into the noble family of Cascurant de Nemours, who has almost agreed to the marriage of her son with . . .

'Come, Germain! . . . It's . . . It's . . .'

There are no words strong enough, to her mind, to express what she feels . . . It's a trap! . . . It's . . . All that is missing are journalists and photographers! . . . And what if she is not allowed to leave, what if her name were to get all over tomorrow's papers? . . .

She can hardly believe she has managed to reach the landing outside with her son in tow, without being detained.

With one forefinger, Maigret presses a few shreds of tobacco into his pipe and takes one last look around the room. Then a nod to Lucas and Janvier.

'Let's be off.'

The little old lady asks if she is going to be left to make her own way home, but he reassures her. No, he hasn't forgotten her . . .

'You, madame, if you will allow me, I shall take home personally, in a taxi . . .'

To her he behaves with the tenderness that one shows only to an aged mother.

9. The Night of Onion Soup

At times like these, there is in Maigret a curious mix of, on the one hand, grossly epicurean self-indulgence and voluptuous surrender to the cravings of the flesh and, on the other, intense cerebral activity and an inner life lived almost to breaking-point.

Despite the storm, the night was warm, and the front windows of the big brasserie on Boulevard de Clichy were wide open. The two men were sitting where the terrace met the bar. On one side a hot, brightly lit bustle, the comings and goings of waiters, the lively groups of diners; on the other, tables deserted under the awning, which bulged with water; two young women with empty glasses in front of them; the rain, which was still falling, but not with the same intensity as earlier. Place Blanche with its electric signs, beyond a patch of darkness where taxis skidded on the wet asphalt, and the glowing reflection of the sails of the Moulin Rouge, which turned tirelessly . . .

Alternating mugginess and cooling breezes, summer's end turning into a Paris autumn and back again . . . The two men had just eaten onion soup with croutons and, after bringing plates of luscious sauerkraut with frankfurters, the waiter was already serving more beers. Strains of music floated in from somewhere. The elderly man did not miss a mouthful, not one whiff of the aroma, not a single second of this special moment, and when he raised his eyes and looked at the inspector, he had an apologetic air.

It was midnight. Just as Lucas was holding the door for the two women to get into the taxi, Maigret had caught him by the sleeve.

'Where are you taking them, you clown?'

'To the cells, sir, just like you told me . . .'

'Take them back to *our* place. I want you and Janvier to keep an eye on them until I get back . . .'

As a result, they had not yet been put with the tarts who were regularly rounded up by the prison van in the usual night raids. They were each given a chair in an empty office in Quai des Orfèvres, where they waited. They were determined not to say anything and sat as stiff-backed as if they were in a drawing room. Except that Antoinette Le Cloaguen's lips moved silently the way old women's lips do behind a pillar in a church, but what she recited to herself was in fact what she intended to say in due course to her lawyer.

The little old lady, Madame Biron, had gone back to the priest's house, where she had been accompanied by Maigret. In the taxi she confided:

'How can it be that one of the good Lord's creatures could do such things?'

That left the old man, whom Maigret had taken out to eat on Boulevard de Clichy. The onion soup and the sauerkraut and frankfurters had sent him into paroxysms of ecstasy.

'Did they feed you badly?'

'They said I didn't have any table manners, they always brought me my grub to eat in my room. Just enough so I didn't starve to death. I was always left with an empty feeling in the pit of my stomach. The daughter wasn't so bad. Sometimes she used to give me something to eat in secret . . .'

'Why didn't you just leave?'

The look the wretched man gave Maigret spoke volumes and needed no comment. It was the look of a man who has been terrorized all his life and cannot conceive that it should occur to anyone to resist their tormentors!

'You don't know what they're like. She treated me so cruelly that there were some evenings I thought she was going to hit me. She used to say that if I told on her, she wouldn't hesitate to kill me. I saw her in Saint-Raphaël when she made me wall up the body. She worked next to me in the cellar, like a man . . . She helped me carry the corpse like it was any old parcel . . .'

'Who killed your daughter, Picard?'

Maigret had let him eat up all his sauerkraut in peace before asking this question in a natural voice, while looking out casually at the sparkling lights on the boulevard and the moving reflection of the sails of the windmill.

'I swear to you, inspector, that it wasn't her . . . I don't know who did it . . . If I knew . . .'

His voice grows muted, as if regretting that this amazing moment should be interrupted so soon with a reminder of that awful event.

'Once, Marie told me . . . Because I always called her Marie . . . Jeanne was just for her clients . . . Once she said

I mustn't go and see her at just any time of day, I had to send a little note to let her know. But I used to go anyway, couldn't help it. I'd wait for a few minutes on the pavement on the opposite side of the road to see if anyone went in . . . That day, she was by herself . . .'

Maigret pauses for a moment, because old Picard has got out the broken-stemmed pipe which he had salvaged from God knows where. And then the inspector, who always keeps two pipes in his pocket, offers him one, without a word. The old man fills it. Women's laughter from a table close by. A man prowls round the terrace, hesitating between the two tarts, whose faces he cannot see.

'She was worried. She said she was having problems because of me and that it could get serious. At one moment, she jumped when she heard a car stop at the kerb and she leaned out over the balcony . . . It was then she pushed me into the kitchen, but I couldn't tell you if she turned the key in the lock . . .'

'So you didn't see the man who came up?'

'No. I vaguely heard them whispering . . .'

'So it was a man?'

'Oh yes . . . But wait . . . Marie did tell me something else . . . I'll try to remember . . . My memory's got terrible . . .'

Maigret orders two brandies and draws on his pipe while he waits.

'Oh yes . . . This is more or less what she said: "I know someone who used to see you on the Côte d'Azur. He comes up to Paris every week and he recognized you one day as you were leaving here . . ."'

Maigret does not react. He inhales the coolness of the

rain, breathes in the Paris night, while his gaze lingers on familiar sights, and in his mind's eye he conjures up other images in extraordinary detail.

This is his best, his greatest time, a time that is his very own, the time which makes up for all the monotonous stages of his investigations . . .

Old Picard, way down south, wandering around Cannes . . .

'Tell me, Picard, how did you end up like this? . . .'

'Dunno . . . I never amounted to much . . . I was a packer in a shoe factory in Caen. My wife left me. Who with, I never found out. I never learned what became of her. I started moving around a lot, working at various jobs, and when I'd get too ground down or too drunk I'd get the first train out to anywhere . . . That's how! . . . Then one day I just stopped working. It was at Cannes . . . When that woman . . .'

The mere thought of her still fills him with terror.

'I was getting on a bit . . . I was losing heart . . . I told myself it sounded like a easy life, that I'd get to sleep in a bed, that I'd have enough to eat . . .'

Then that simple, guileless look returned, and he asked:

'Do you really think she would have killed me?'

'I don't know, Picard, but it's possible . . .'

Maigret follows the thought through . . . The old man, who knew all about being poor and was sick of it, had been ready to sell himself for a little security . . . Antoinette Le Cloaguen had never known poverty but was so afraid of it that in order to provide for her old age and build up a certain sum of money on which she had fixed as her goal with cold calculation, she had been capable of . . .

'Right! . . . It's time . . . Waiter! . . . Bill, please!'

The people all round them live life as it is. They inhabit the present moment. But Maigret lives three, five, ten lives at the same time: he is in Cannes, in Saint-Raphaël, on Boulevard des Batignolles and in Rue Coulaincourt . . .

Both of them are now outside, in the rain. The old man asks with disarming candour:

'Where are we going?'

'Listen, Picard, would you mind very much, for just one more night, sleeping in a cell at the Police Judiciaire?'

'Are they there?'

'No . . . In the morning I'll send someone to get you . . . We will come . . .'

'If you like . . .'

'Taxi . . . Police Judiciaire . . .'

The dark banks of the river. The red light over the entrance to the cells of the Police Judiciaire . . .

'Good night, Picard . . . I'll see you tomorrow . . . Sergeant! . . . Will you take care of this man? . . .'

The duty officer who takes the old man off to a small room to be searched has not the slightest inkling of the fact that only shortly before his prisoner had been having a late supper with the inspector in a brasserie on Boulevard de Clichy.

There is light in only two windows of police headquarters. Maigret pictures mother and daughter sitting, Lucas yawning, and Janvier who will almost certainly have sent out for beer and sandwiches. Should he go up? . . . Should he . . . ?

Maigret strides along the riverbank, then stops and leans

briefly on his elbows on the parapet. There is only a fine drizzle falling now, and it feels cool on his brow.

Odd thoughts . . . Of course! . . . The clairvoyant was expecting her fate, or at least trouble . . . She spoke of a man who 'came up to Paris' every week, and the expression itself describes the kind of individual involved very clearly . . .

On Friday, a car had stopped outside . . . The green convertible in all likelihood . . .

Maigret is now at the Pont-Neuf. An empty taxi drives past.

'Rue Coulaincourt . . .'

'What number?'

'I'll stop you . . .'

He could leave it until tomorrow. It would be more lawful. What he is about to do is frankly irregular, but it wouldn't be the first time. And anyway do criminals worry about legality?

He can't see himself going to bed and waiting for the morning. He has nothing else to do. He is raring to go . . .

'One moment . . . A little further up, on the left . . . The shop with a white front . . .'

He tells the driver to wait and rings a doorbell. He has to ring three times, though the first ring seems to make enough noise inside the sleeping building to wake the dead. At length, there is a click that releases the door lock. He pushes it open and feels for the time-switch. He raps on the window of the concierge's lodge.

'Excuse me, where will I find the people who run the dairy . . .'

'What is it? . . . What's the matter? . . .'

Eventually she is wide awake and appears, a strange face topped with curlers . . .

'I want to speak to the people who run the dairy . . . What's that? . . . They sleep behind the shop? Isn't there a bell? . . . And what about their serving girl, Emma?'

Good! It's on the seventh floor, where the owners of the dairy rent a maid's room for her.

'Thank you, madame . . . Don't worry. I won't make a noise . . .'

After the third floor, he fails to locate a time-switch and makes the rest of his way up using matches. Seventh floor, third door along, he'd been told. He knocks gently. He puts one ear to the door. He hears a release of breath like a sigh and then the sound of a body, presumably snug and warm, turning over heavily in a bed.

He knocks again. A clogged voice:

'What's the matter?'

He speaks in a whisper for fear of waking the neighbours:

'Open the door . . . It's me, Detective Chief Inspector Maigret . . .'

Bare feet on a wooden floor. The light goes on, more footsteps, comings and goings. Eventually in the half-opened door appears a sturdy girl in a nightdress, with scared eyes and features still furred by sleep.

'What do you want?'

The atmosphere smells of the night, of a woman, of a warm, moist bed, with an underlying redolence of face powder and soapy water.

'What do you want?'

He shuts the door behind him. Emma slips an old coat over her nightdress through whose flimsy material her large sawdust-doll figure is vaguely discernible.

'He's been arrested . . .'

'Who?'

'The murderer . . . The man in the green convertible . . .'

'What did you say? . . .'

She is slow to gather her wits. Her eyes grow steadily more confused.

'He's just been arrested . . . I need you to come to Quai des Orfèvres and identify him . . .'

'Oh my God!'

'Get dressed. There's nothing to be afraid of. I'll turn and face the wall . . .'

He hears her moving around behind him, searching through the pile of underwear on a chair and looking for her stockings under the bed.

'Oh my God! . . . Oh my God! . . .' she goes on repeating.

She is crying, sniffling quietly. Over and over she repeats: 'Oh my God!' Then:

'How is it possible? . . .'

He turns round while she is still in her pink slip fastening her stockings. Oh, he has seen it all before! Even she forgets that she is in the middle of getting dressed in the presence of a man.

'You will recognize him, won't you?'

'Will I have to look him in the face, speak to him?'

And then she flings herself on the bed and starts sobbing, shaking her head, saying over and over:

'No, I don't want to! . . . I don't want to! . . . It was my fault you arrested him! . . .'

If only a photographer had been there at that moment to take a picture of Maigret, a hulking figure standing in this room which is too small for him, leaning over a fat girl in her slip, as he taps her on the shoulder! . . .

'Calm down, Emma . . . Come on . . . It's time to go . . .'

She bites the sheets. She continues to shake her head as if she has made up her mind to cling fast to the bed, in desperation.

'You have been silly enough as it is . . . If I hadn't stepped in, you would be in prison too by this time . . .'

The magic word sobers her up immediately, and she looks up:

'Prison?'

'Yes, and put away for a long time. Because what you did may well be considered as aiding and abetting. Why didn't you recognize him when I showed you all those photos?'

She bites her lower lip until it bleeds, her expression becomes more obstinate.

'Well? . . . Answer me: why?'

'Because I love him!'

'And meanwhile we have been wasting our time. He might have got away with it! . . . We might have arrested an innocent man! Get dressed. Don't make me call the police officer who's waiting downstairs . . .'

It is a strange couple who make their way in silence down the dark stairs. The taxi is still waiting.

'Get in.'

And in the car, Emma's pensive voice:

'Why did he kill her? . . . She was his mistress, wasn't she? . . . She had other men . . . He was jealous . . .'

'Perhaps . . .'

'I'm sure that's why . . . He loved her . . .'

She follows him up the steps into the Police Judiciaire and then along the high, wide corridor, where only one lamp is lit to serve as a night light. Hearing a noise, Janvier emerges from an office and is astonished to see the chief there at this hour with the girl who delivers the milk.

'What are they doing now?' asks Maigret.

'The daughter is asleep. The other one is waiting.'

Maigret walks into his office, tells Emma to come in and then closes the door.

'Where is he?'

'Hold on a moment. You'll see him soon enough. Sit down.'

Poor fat girl, usually so rosy-cheeked and now, tonight, so ashen as to be almost as pale as the moon.

'Right . . . When you came here the first time, because your employers had told you to, these are the photos I showed you. Is that correct? . . .'

He does not hold out the entire pile, but lays them out one by one. He gives them names, all in no particular order:

'Tattoo Justin . . . Bébert from Montpellier . . . La Caille . . .'

He is the more tense of the pair of them, because everything now depends on this moment. He does not dare look the girl in the face. He has found a way of not scaring her off: he keeps watching her hands with their podgy fingers and broken nails. One of them is resting down on his desk and the other seems as if it is ready to pounce on the tell-tale photo.

'Little Louis, from Belleville . . . Justin . . .'

He stops breathing, then suddenly his chest swells, at last he can gulp down air and escape that painful paralysis, for the two hands have twitched and closed with one single jerk.

'This is him, isn't it? . . . Justin . . . Justin from Toulon . . .'

She shivers as if grown suddenly cold. She looks up, and the expression on her face changes, but is all wide-eyed innocence when she asks:

'You didn't know! . . . Where is he?'

At last she understands, her anger rises, she seems ready to throw herself at the inspector.

'It wasn't true! . . . You haven't arrested him! . . . You laid a trap for me and it was me who . . . it was me . . . it was me . . . me! . . .'

'Calm down, Emma . . . Calm down . . . Take it from me, Justin is an extremely nasty piece of work . . .'

'It was me . . . me! . . .'

'Come now . . . You're tired . . . You have to be up early . . . I'll get a car to take you home . . .'

He rings for Janvier.

'Take this young lady home . . . Go easy on her . . . And if there's anything left in the drinks cupboard, pour her a small glass of something to make her feel better . . .'

Still, she is the lucky one: she wouldn't have got off so lightly if Justin had taken more of an interest in her!

10. *The Honest Dishonest Man*

'Hello? . . . Police Judiciaire? . . . It's Madame Maigret . . . Is my husband there?'

'Of course I am, sweetheart . . .'

'Aren't you coming home tonight? . . .'

'No. Maybe tomorrow? . . . It depends . . .'

Kindly, long-suffering Madame Maigret, who has woken with a start at four in the morning and is worried when she realizes there is an empty space next to her.

'No . . . I won't be going away . . . Just a shortish trip . . . Sleep tight! . . .'

Alone in his office, he works through a whole series of phone calls and begins to feel like the conductor of an orchestra.

'Sorry, detective chief inspector . . . Mascouvin will be in no fit state to be questioned for another three or four days . . .'

Next, branches of the Sûreté, first Toulon, then Nice.

'Justin, yes . . . Whatever it takes? . . . Understood! . . .'

Going through the police station nearest to Rue Notre-Dame-de-Lorette, he contacts Torrence, who is still watching Monsieur Blaise's apartment.

He is on his way! . . . No, perhaps not quite on his way . . . Peeping through the keyhole, he first relishes the sight of Madame Le Cloaguen sitting ramrod straight on her chair while the all-too-casual Lucas has dropped off and is snoring.

Day is breaking. The air still smells damp, but it has stopped raining, and the ground is littered with leaves and debris.

'Hey! . . . Taxi! . . . Is your tank full enough for a longish trip? . . .'

Eight o'clock. Antoinette Le Cloaguen, looking tired and drawn, but with her dignity intact, is speaking to Lucas, who has got up and is washing his face at the drinking fountain in the alcove.

'Is your inspector intending to keep us here for much longer?'

'If you'd rather go straight to jail . . .'

'I think I would prefer that!'

Her daughter's hair flops down over one cheek. Janvier has managed a couple of hours' sleep on a sofa in the waiting room. The Police Judiciaire is starting to wake up.

At nine, all the inspectors meet in the office of the commissioner of the Police Judiciaire to give their daily reports. Only Maigret is absent.

'Any of you gentlemen know what's going on?'

He reads out a message received by phone from the Sûreté at Nice, reporting that a certain Justin has been arrested at the Promenade Pier Casino, or more specifically just as he was leaving it, at seven this morning. The man protests his innocence.

'It's probably for Maigret.'

'Is he not in his office?'

The commissioner opens a door and is surprised to find two women who look as if they have spent the night there. They are being guarded by a rather sour Lucas. He offers a perfunctory greeting:

'Ladies . . .'

But he beats a hasty retreat when he sees the older of the two spring to her feet and bear down on him.

'Who was that man?'

Lucas replies:

'The man in charge . . .'

'Tell him that I demand . . . that I want . . .'

'Can't be done! . . . . It's time for morning reports . . .'

A Paris taxi is driving through the mud of a cart track between Morsang and Fontainebleau, or more precisely between the locks at Morsang and Citanguette. It has now stopped outside two small inns.

'Tell me,' says Maigret to the landlord of one of them, 'would you by any chance . . .'

He holds up a number of photographs, and one in particular . . . A shake of the head . . . Maigret drains a small glass . . .

Look! A tree has been blown down by the storm and is lying across the lane. A team of roadmen is already there, and they have started wielding axes.

'Tell me, boys . . .'

They stare in amazement at this man with mud on his boots who smokes pipe after pipe to help him to stay awake.

Eventually, one of the men says:

'This one, I'm sure . . . Almost every Sunday, near the sandpit, with a car that . . .'

It's the third time the examining magistrate has phoned Maigret's office.

'No, sir . . . he's not back yet but he called to say he'll be here in a quarter of an hour . . . Yes . . . Monsieur Blaise? . . . He's in another office with Inspector Torrence . . . He wants to speak to the minister . . . Yes . . . No, I don't know . . . The wife? Still carrying on about the same thing . . . I have indeed, I had coffee and croissants sent up for them . . . The mother drank the coffee but she wouldn't touch the croissants . . .'

Everyone is waiting for Maigret. The commissioner is not at all happy, he is getting complaints from all sides. Mademoiselle Berthe, whom the inspector has called in by a pneumatic telegram, has arrived in her little red hat and is waiting patiently in the antechamber.

They would all be very surprised, including old Picard on his bench in the cells of the Police Judiciaire, if they could only see the inspector now.

He is literally slumped in the back of a taxi. His eyes are closed. No, not shut. Just closed enough for him to see the passing landscape as a blur of wet, dripping foliage.

He smokes his pipe. He turns things over in his mind. He plays a strange game in which human beings are counters and each counter has to be put in its proper place.

It's really quite simple! But it's also very complicated at the same time! Damn that nuisance Mascouvin for being a fly in the ointment!

His feelings are not charitable towards Mascouvin, who, bandaged up to the eyeballs, is still at the Hôtel-Dieu . . . If it hadn't been for him . . .

Yet at the same time Maigret feels very indulgent towards him . . . Could this be on account of the girl with the dimples, that nice Mademoiselle Berthe? . . .

So simple! . . .

To see the full picture, he had only to understand Mascouvin, *the honest dishonest man* who stumbled once and is haunted by remorse . . .

All he had to do was to proceed like an accountant by adding up receipts and outgoings: what the clerk earned at Proud and Drouin on the one side, and what he spent bringing up Mademoiselle Berthe and settling her in her flat on the other . . .

What he earned would not have been enough . . .

And Monsieur Drouin had stated categorically: his clerk had not been in a position to steal money from the till.

With every bump and rut, Maigret is shaken, and his pipe twitches between his teeth, but he does not lose the thread of what he intends to say to them later, in his office on Quai des Orfèvres, when all of them, all the counters, are assembled . . .

'Yes, sir,' he will say to the examining magistrate, 'that's where it all started . . . Mascouvin was tempted . . . Tempted by whom? . . . By one of his firm's clients, a man who dealt only on a small scale himself but took a keen interest in all the other business transacted there . . . Because, you must understand, this man, Monsieur Blaise, is the most evil and intelligent of all blackmailers . . .

'My, my! What a set-up he created! He has accomplices and yet he is never seen to associate with anyone! No one comes to his apartment in Rue Notre-Dame-de-Lorette, where he is regarded as the very model of a rich man who does not have to work for a living . . .

'At Morsang, at the Beau Pigeon, he is a keen angler who does not mix with the other guests . . .

'He fishes for pike . . . He fishes for them in the tall reeds on the left bank, where he is hidden from view . . .'

And as recently as this morning, Isidore was forced to confess to Maigret:

'What do you want me to say. He used to go off to see a married woman somewhere. I don't know who. I never saw her. He didn't want it to look obvious so he asked me to catch fish for him so that . . .'

So who was it then who came to meet him there, between the locks at Morsang and Citanguette?

Let's see . . . Who does Monsieur Blaise, a careful man, who never appears in person in any of his shady dealings, need? He needs a strong-arm man . . .

In other words, Justin! . . . Justin shuttles between the Côte d'Azur and Paris. His job is to make 'clients' understand that if they don't 'cough up' . . .

Justin, the man in the green convertible . . .

Who else does Monsieur Blaise need? People to supply information about more or less dodgy business deals which are done . . .

And that is how Mascouvin, honest Mascouvin, was tempted . . . He is a clerk with a financial services firm which processes, among others, large-scale land development schemes and compulsory purchase orders in which town councillors and others receive . . .

Don't you understand, Monsieur Drouin? You were quite correct in saying that it is absolutely impossible for a clerk employed by you to steal a thousand-franc note. But what about copies of compromising letters? . . .

That is what Mascouvin supplied! That is where he got the money to set his sister up in her own place and in one for himself, to pay for . . .

From then on, there is no going back. Henceforth, someone has a hold over him. He is the honest dishonest man who strayed once from the straight and narrow and is doomed to be dishonest for the rest of his life.

And how he suffers for it . . . He suffers too from the indifference of the countess, with whom he has fallen in love . . .

He is a worrier, a very complicated man . . . Monsieur Drouin said it . . . He is a man who believes he is constantly under suspicion, for whom everything he touches goes wrong in the end . . .

'What?' he replies, still anticipating the examining magistrate's questions. 'Is there something else? . . .'

Maigret raps on the glass panel between him and the driver. They are just entering Paris. Still some way off, on Quai des Orfèvres, they are all waiting for him.

'Stop here a moment, driver . . . I'm thirsty.'

Actually, the truth is that he needs a little more time to prepare his verbal report.

'But what about Mademoiselle Jeanne, the clairvoyant?' the magistrate will ask.

'An accomplice . . .' Maigret will say.

'Whose accomplice?'

'A confederate, if you like, one of Monsieur Blaise's partners in crime. What better informant is there for a blackmailer than an extra-far-sighted clairvoyant? Clients leak all their secrets to her in the questions they ask her about their future. Those secrets, not always pure as the driven snow, are extracted with the aid of the crystal ball, collected every week by Justin, the man in the green convertible, passed over by him at Morsang and used by Monsieur Blaise, the mastermind . . . Now do you understand, sir?

'What's that? . . . How did Mademoiselle Jeanne . . . That I couldn't say . . . Don't forget that her mother went to the bad and that her father ended up a tramp, that she'd tried to make a go of her life and that she made some bad choices. Did she fall for Justin's good looks? Or was she in the racket just for the money?

'We'll find others, you'll see, people who sold secrets for cash to Monsieur Blaise, from which he made large profits.

'And then Justin recognizes the man posing as Le Cloaguen and uncovers the mystery of the house on Boulevard des Batignolles . . .

'A solid gold opportunity! Madame Le Cloaguen will *cough up*! She is the ideal victim! . . . They'll make her pay through the nose if she wants to keep her income of 200,000 francs coming in . . .'

Maigret is sitting at a table near the counter of the small bistro, and the driver begins to wonder if he hasn't gone to sleep.

'That, I am sure, sir, is how it all happened . . . When Mademoiselle Jeanne learned they were going to blackmail Madame Le Cloaguen and that in the process her father would get into trouble, she perhaps begged, then threatened, to go to the police and expose the whole gang . . .

'*It was then that they decided to kill the clairvoyant!*

'Do you see it all now? Without realizing it, she gave them a fantastic target on a plate! Through her, they'd get their hands on a goose that laid golden eggs . . . How much would they demand from Madame Le Cloaguen? Two hundred thousand francs to start with? . . . One full year of the annuity paid to the bogus ex-ship's doctor?

'But it's no go. Mademoiselle Jeanne won't play, so they get rid of her . . .

'You know, sir, it's actually very difficult to find people who are *crooked to the core*, if I can put it that way.

'She was like Mascouvin, not crooked enough . . .

'Monsieur Blaise's speciality is using what we at Police HQ call the *small fry* . . .

'And so the clairvoyant will die at five in the afternoon.'

At Police Headquarters, people are getting impatient. The examining magistrate has left his own office and moved into Maigret's. The driver of the inspector's taxi is also getting impatient because he has been 'on' all night and would very much like to get to bed.

'Give me another calva . . .'

They will kill her! The gang will kill her! Poor Mascouvin knows! He has been told all about it, perhaps to tighten the hold they have on him! He looks for a way of stopping it happening, whatever the cost . . .

Picture him in his usual café on Place de la République . . .

Maigret seethes with anger! He clenches his fists with rage! Because if that man hadn't been so complicated . . .

Obviously, he can hardly be expected to go to the police and say:

'I'm part of a gang of extortionists. At five o'clock tomorrow afternoon we're going to murder a clairvoyant whose name and address I don't know.'

He tries to think of a way, his brain works overtime, he devises plans and comes up with the business with the blotter, which will keep him out of the picture. To shield himself from the revenge of his accomplices, he even concocts the theft of the thousand-franc note, which will mean that he will be kept safely locked up for some time . . .

'And there, sir, you have it!'

Picpus! Ha! Ha! Mascouvin is about to sign when, gazing vaguely around, he spots a jovial smiling face on a fairground strong man who is carrying a mirror-fronted wardrobe around . . .

Signed, Picpus . . .

And when he learns that the deed has been done, all the fool can think of is committing suicide.

'Excuse me! . . .'

The chauffeur shakes his fare, who has fallen asleep at his table. Maigret opens his eyes blearily.

'Where do you want me to take you?'

'Quai des Orfèvres.'

'What? . . .'

'Police Judiciaire . . .'

He had been deeply asleep. What is left of the distance to his destination is not long enough for him to come fully awake. As far as he is concerned, the Picpus case is solved. But now the hard work starts: to explain it to the examining magistrate and then . . .

Suddenly, he gives a start. The image of Madame Le Cloaguen comes back to him, and he most definitely, it must be said, has it in for her. If there had been no Monsieur Blaise and no murder in Rue Coulaincourt, she would have gone on with her sordid little scheme. She would have continued to rake in 200,000 francs every year until the old tramp's death and all that time she wouldn't let him smoke and would bolt the door to his room!

'What a bitch! . . .'

The Police Judiciaire building . . . It is a grim Maigret who climbs the stairs.

'Everybody's there, waiting for you, detective chief inspector . . .'

'I know . . . I know . . .'

It is now noon. Everyone is waiting for him, and they are all annoyed with him, even and especially the examining magistrate, who considers that his dignity . . .

Maigret's exposition of his conclusions lasts until three.

'You'll have to prove it,' jeers Monsieur Blaise.

'We have proof . . . Justin has been questioned by the Nice police . . .'

It's true. In the end, they made Justin 'spill' by threatening to throw the book at him, and, as happens so often, he loaded the blame on Blaise in the hope of being allowed to claim extenuating circumstances.

'Aren't you coming home yet?' Madame Maigret says into the phone.

'I'll be there in . . . say an hour . . . What's for dinner? . . .'

Just one more small thing to do. The examining magistrate has pointed out that before proceeding against Madame Le Cloaguen the victim must press charges.

The victim is the Argentinian who originally arranged to pay an annuity of 200,000 francs to the man who saved his daughter's life.

It turns out he is dead.

Like many South American heiresses, his daughter has married a foreign prince and lives in Paris.

A footman in knee-length breeches shows Maigret into a sumptuous drawing room in a grand town house off the Champs-Élysées and waits. He waits for an hour. Poor Madame Maigret! He is kept waiting for another hour and falls asleep again.

'You must forgive me, detective chief inspector . . . They forgot to let me know you were here . . . though I can't think . . .'

The girl who had once been saved by Dr Le Cloaguen is now a woman of fifty who dresses like a damsel and is certain to be one of the best customers in all the beauty parlours. She is escorted by a young man who performs the role of attendant knight.

'I wanted to ask . . . You may remember that your father,

a long time ago, arranged for an annuity of 200,000 francs to be paid to a doctor who . . .'

'Oh yes . . . When I had yellow fever . . . Can you believe it, José, I caught yellow fever and . . .'

'The beneficiary is dead and . . .'

'Poor thing! . . . He must still have been a young man . . .'

'Actually, he was . . .'

Careful! It would not do to mention age in this house! . . .

'His wife . . . To avoid losing the annuity . . . She found a tramp hanging around the port at Cannes who looked like her husband . . .'

'Oh, how priceless! Heavens, José, it's perfectly priceless! Tell me, inspector, did she . . . you know . . . with her tramp? . . . What I mean is did she behave as if the tramp was really her husband, and did they have children? . . .'

'Given the fact that we're dealing with a swindle of which you are the victim, I am here to ask if you wish to press charges and if . . .'

'Press charges? Why would I do that?'

'Because you have been defrauded annually for the past ten years of a sum of . . .'

'Poor woman! If she had only written to me. I'd forgotten all about this annuity. I leave all that to the accountants. I have no wish to . . . Inspector, tell me, it would be so amusing to meet a woman who . . . It's too priceless! . . . Another husband but just the same . . . José, don't you think it's perfectly thrilling? Tell her to ring me and fix a time for her to come here for tea and . . .'

*

'At last! There you are, Maigret! I was beginning to think . . . I've made the veal fricandeau just as you asked me to over the phone.'

But the inspector, as soon as he is in the hall, removes his jacket, tie and collar and mumbles:

'Must sleep . . .'

'What? Aren't you going to eat? You . . .'

He is not listening. He makes a bee-line for his bedroom and sighs as he undresses:

'Too stupid! . . . You know, people are just too stupid for words . . .'

He makes the bed-springs creak, wrestles with his pillow to make a hollow for his head and, already half-asleep, mutters:

'Still, if they weren't so stupid, there'd be no need for policemen . . .'

INSPECTOR MAIGRET

OTHER TITLES IN THE SERIES

LOCK N° 1
GEORGES SIMENON

'There was amusement in Ducrau's eyes. In the inspector's too. They stood looking at each other with the same stifled mirth which was full of unspoken thoughts, perhaps of defiance and maybe too of an odd respect.'

A man hauled out of the Charenton canal one night; a girl wandering, confused, in a white nightdress … these events draw Maigret into the world of the charismatic self-made businessman Ducrau, and the misdeeds of his past.

Translated by David Coward

OTHER TITLES IN THE SERIES

MAIGRET
GEORGES SIMENON

'It was indeed Maigret who was beside him, smoking his pipe, his velvet collar upturned, his hat perched on his head. But it wasn't an enthusiastic Maigret. It wasn't even a Maigret who was sure of himself.'

Maigret's peaceful retirement in the country is interrupted when his nephew comes to him for help after being implicated in a crime he didn't commit. Soon Maigret is back in the heart of Paris, and out of place in a once-familiar world...

Translated by Ros Schwartz

OTHER TITLES IN THE SERIES

CÉCILE IS DEAD
GEORGES SIMENON

'Barely twenty-eight years old. But it would be difficult to look more like an old maid, to move less gracefully, no matter how hard she tried to be pleasing. Those black dresses . . . that ridiculous green hat!'

For six months the dowdy Cécile has been coming to the police station, desperate to convince them that someone has been breaking into her aunt's apartment. No one takes her seriously – until Maigret unearths a story of merciless, deep-rooted greed.

Translated by Anthea Bell

OTHER TITLES IN THE SERIES

And more to follow